An Ancient Whisper

ADVENTURES WITH DANIEL

— BOOK TWO —

KAREN ALEXANDER

To Andi who has always been my spiritual midwife.
To Brent who never, ever gives up.
To Bodhi who faces the world while I dive deep.
To Daniel, my joy.
Many, many thanks.

Prologue

Out of nothing, and all things, fire creeps silently into form. Fragments of purple, red and silver rise, and find their way again to the surface. A new heart begins to flicker, pulse, and turn with love.

"Come my sweet being...it is time..."

Strands of spiraled light come together in joy. Unseen hands sweep along them, weaving a glorious new form out of a passion known only in this place.

"Come, my love...it is time..."

The heart spins faster now, its purpose to reflect the radiant face of the one who created it. Light flows into it, then outward from it, sending sparkling particles of silver and gold dancing across an incandescent plain.

"It is time..."

Sweet murmurs of indescribable love become beads of turquoise and amber and attach themselves to the strands of the new form. Each one contains a memory of this place and enough love to fuel its existence through the coming journey.

"Oh, but I never want to leave you..."

The new heart flutters with sorrow at the necessary parting, while gentle hands caress the form, sending comfort and under-standing sweeping through the strands of light. Soft, lingering kisses find every corner of this creation, giving reassurance that there is truly no end and never can be.

"Now, my love...now, it is time."

An Ancient Whisper

*Now it began to glow, then radiate a soft
violet light. Unable to move my feet, I was
mesmerized by the sight. The gentle song grew
louder, and the dumpster began to disappear,
replaced by swimming particles of silver and
blue. My eyes were wide with shock, and
my heart sped along at an impossible rate.
I looked in awe as the dumpster vanished,
replaced by a luminous doorway.*

♥

One

Locked in a diligent embrace with a dark blue dumpster, the rumpled man never noticed me.

Feeling an involuntary wave of revulsion, I watched him pull something from the receptacle and furtively stuff it into his dirty tweed coat. Tall, and almost thin enough to see through, he reached deep into mounds of pungent cardboard boxes in a dedicated search for food.

I walked by, silently judging myself. My shoes clicking along the sidewalk, I wondered how we could call ourselves civilized and not provide care for those who obviously needed it. What a paradox it was. This man had to dig for his life in refuse while there was a top-notch restaurant right around the corner. My mind immediately provided the customary argument: he might be dangerous. After all, it was after nine o'clock. It was dark out here. I decided that the next time I wanted to go out for dinner; I'd go at an earlier time.

Glancing up the block, I saw the man again. How did he get up ahead of me? Now standing under a street light, long unwashed hair hanging limply across his face, the homeless man gazed back at me. Uneasy, I refused to meet his eyes and directed my attention to the sidewalk. When I looked up, he was gone.

Gathering my coat closer to my body, I tried to shut out the chill of the new wind. The evening was so clear; I could see the hills and valleys on the bright, full moon. I stopped for a moment and gazed at the canopy of sparkling stars overhead. Nights like this could make me feel so small and so gigantic at the same time. The universe stretched outwards from this sidewalk into an immense expanse that nobody, not even the scientists, could grasp. And yet, I knew I was vast as well. I didn't always know that, but recent events had driven the idea well into my consciousness.

There he was again. An unwelcome anxiety stirred in my stomach. I could see the tall figure, this time fussing through a wire trash container. My car was parked in the next block. I decided to simply walk past him with determined self-confidence. But, expecting that he would ask me for money, I decided what I would give.

A deep breath reminded me to relax and forget my preoccupation with the dreaded "might be's," "could happens" that my mind insisted on producing with profound efficiency.

I was within six feet of him when he stopped his search through the refuse. Here we go, I thought, tightening my fingers around the bills in my pocket.

"Good evening," he said in a surprisingly pleasant baritone.

"Good evening," I replied, hoping to convey my sense of urgency and thus, not spark an unwanted conversation.

Without invitation, the stranger began walking along side me. Though his face was covered in a raw, uneven bristle, it was not what I had expected. Shocking in its beauty, the streetlights illuminated a strong jaw, aquiline nose, and handsome mouth.

"Boise is an interesting place," he said quietly.

"Yes, it is," I replied without enthusiasm, again hoping to dissuade his apparent interest in me.

"Up ahead...that's where I stay most of the time." The deep voice sounded like it had been educated.

"Have you been in Boise a long time?" I answered politely. The fear I had tried to argue away began to rise within me. He showed no sign that he intended to leave me alone.

"Not so long," he said softly, his steps only matching my quickened pace. "But up ahead, that's where I stay most of the time."

Heart pounding, I blurted, "Well, you know, I think I've gone past my turn." I wheeled around and started off in the opposite direction. Why wasn't there anyone else on the street? My hands clenched in my coat pocket, and I prepared to run for safety.

Sure enough, he turned and followed me. In a friendly tone he stated, "Well, I can show you the place that I stay going this direction if you like."

I decided to stop avoiding the problem and faced him squarely. "Look, you seem like a nice guy, but I'm in a hurry and I really don't have time to go with you. Besides, how can you show me the same thing going one way that you can going the completely opposite direction?"

In the darkness, he suddenly reached out his hand. My body stiffened with frightened expectation. But his touch on my forearm was gentle. I looked into his face, searching for an explanation for his intent. I could find nothing there except a look of expectation.

"Do you need money? Is that what this is about?" I asked, my voice a little louder than I had meant it to.

"You know, everything isn't about money," he said calmly. "I just want a moment of your time, that's all."

"Why?" The question was stupid, but I could think of nothing else to say.

Suddenly, he laughed, perfect white teeth in surprising juxtaposition with his unkempt face. His blue eyes crinkled, and the amusement seemed to rise from deep inside him. "There is nothing to be afraid of," he said. "I have no need and no reason to cause you harm. I wish I could say the same thing about what people have in mind for me."

His face suddenly looked sad, and he added, "Do you have any idea how mean-spirited people can be when you don't look like they do?"

I was feeling guilty underneath my uneasiness. "It must be really hard," I offered.

"Sometimes," he replied quietly. "Watching people twist

themselves into a knot over something they don't understand is very, very sad."

That's interesting, I thought. I had expected a fervent soliloquy about being the victim of society. A statement of compassion for the middle class was most unusual.

"You know, they really only harm themselves with that fear. They cut themselves off from their own caring hearts. That's a very sad thing."

I had unconsciously turned myself back around toward the direction of my car. Walking rapidly, I said, "You have an interesting perspective. I mean, you seem to care about the people who treat you badly."

"Well, that's not so difficult," he chuckled. "I just try to see beyond their behavior. You know, people, even cruel ones, are mostly just very scared inside. The next thing you know, they're behaving like cretins."

My mind noted the use of the word "cretin." He must have had some education, I thought. Or maybe he managed to read out here.

"Well," he interrupted my ruminations. "Here it is. This is where I stay most of the time."

I looked out over the street and saw nothing but an empty dark sidewalk and another dark blue dumpster. "I'm sorry, I don't understand."

"Right there," he pointed. "That's where I stay." I followed his direction, and my attention could find nothing but the refuse container.

"In there?" I asked sharply. Then, quickly trying to cover up my unintentional rudeness, I added, "Isn't that terribly uncomfortable?"

"I'll show you," he replied with an odd tone.

Grateful I was not being asked to go down an alley, I willingly approached the dumpster. Tapping the unforgiving metal with my knuckles, I tried to be polite. "Don't you get cold?"

The man began to laugh once again, "Oh, Karen! For heaven's sake, don't you know who I am?"

Stunned that he knew my name, I stared at him unable to reply. A familiar lullaby wafted up from the dumpster and I slowly turned to follow the sound.

Now it began to glow, then radiate a soft violet light. Unable to move my feet, I was mesmerized by the sight. The gentle song grew louder, and the dumpster began to disappear, replaced by swimming particles of silver and blue. My eyes were wide with shock, and my heart sped along at an impossible rate. I looked in awe as the dumpster vanished, replaced by a luminous doorway.

The man stood in that doorway, now clean and clear and impossibly beautiful. He extended his hands toward me, and gently said, "Come, let me show you where I stay."

A feeling of tremendous warmth washed over me, and my mind surrendered. Glancing down, I saw that my own body had all but disappeared. I was now comprised of spinning spirals of purple and gold light. My hands were no longer present in their usual form but had become intricate strands of gold and silver.

Two

Mouth ajar, I continued to stare at the man, watching his body dissolve in the swirling light and then emerge again. He smiled and beckoned. Suddenly, nothing made sense to me except to follow him.

Stepping into the doorway, I lost my feet and began to float like a petal of a daisy caught on a gentle breeze. I looked back a last time toward the ordinary street. It was now almost obscured by flowing currents of sparkling violet light.

A feeling of tremendous warmth washed over me, and my mind surrendered. Glancing down, I saw that my own body had all but disappeared. I was now comprised of spinning spirals of purple and gold light. My hands were no longer present in their usual form but had become intricate strands of gold and silver.

"Where are we going?" I asked weakly.

"Nowhere you haven't been before," the mysterious man answered as he turned and walked away from me.

I had no feet to move but simply followed him with a wish. Soon, there was nothing to see but the most glorious shimmering light. "Where? Where am I?" I asked again. Curiously, a sense of profound peace had entered my being.

"You know where you are, Karen. Just let yourself enjoy."

I had learned from Daniel that it was useless to protest when spirit decided to show you something. Wait a minute! "Daniel! Is that you?"

A chuckle emerged from the man's back as he continued his mysterious journey through the light. "Of course it's me. Who else would it be?"

Like a child grasping her mother or father, I launched myself and hugged him. Joy surged through me without restraint. "Daniel, I'm so glad to see you! Where have you been? You're all grown up!"

He stopped, turned, and looked at me with an, "Oh, come on now" expression—the one people give you when you ask about something you already have the answer for.

Daniel had seemed like any other seven-year-old boy when I had met him on an airplane seven months ago. I had dreaded the idea of spending time strapped next to him on the flight to Seattle. But shortly after takeoff, Daniel had removed me from the plane in midair. Miraculously, I had stood safely in the clouds, and watched it disappear.

In an amazing series of adventures, he had taken me places no one had ever seen before and shown me things I never even dreamed of. He had been exhilarating, annoying, and captivating. He had managed to produce the greatest anxiety and the greatest joy in me that it was possible for one poor human to experience. Daniel had shattered all of my cherished beliefs and replaced them with truths which could not be argued.

Who was he? He had refused to answer me directly, always saying it was more important that I know who I was. I had thought he was an angel, but he had denied it. Clearly, he was a spiritual messenger. He had told me that his mission was to remind humanity about its true nature and its purpose on Earth. He had shown me that I was a precious creation of my own soul. I had journeyed into the arms of that soul, even into the realm of heaven itself. And, I had been undeniably changed.

"You know," I said ruefully, "you turned my whole life upside down!"

"You turned it upside down, Karen," he reminded me. "You always have free will."

"As if I could ignore what happened," I protested. I had

returned from my otherworldly experiences and tried to tell my husband and friends about Daniel, and what he had shown me. Their reactions were predictable. Although they tried to be supportive and understanding, I could sense that they all thought I had gone around the bend.

It's funny how people start to speak very slowly when they think you've lost your mind. I'd noticed that a lot in my work as a counselor. Family members would whisper about a client as though he was hearing impaired and wouldn't grasp the fact that they were asking me to hospitalize him. Then, when it came time to speak to their father, son, mother or daughter, their voice would rise well beyond normal speech and words would stretch out as if to be sure all the space was filled so the person would never have a chance to defend himself.

Daniel had warned me. I remembered his little face turning suddenly serious as he said, "It will be hard for you to come back to an ordinary life once you've seen the whole thing!" He was right. It had been very hard. There were so many things that demanded my attention, but I had been having a hard time concentrating on them. I still had my counseling practice, but my heart really wasn't in it. I had seen so many amazing things in the spiritual world; it was terribly difficult to forget about them and try to live an ordinary life again. I had come to understand why mystics retreated to a mountain top.

I hadn't asked for any of this. When I had gotten on that airplane, I had a normal life—friends, spouse, profession, and very little interest in anything which could be considered 'spiritually unusual.' Since that fateful meeting, I had been consumed with what Daniel had shown me. Finding that nobody believed my story, I had stopped talking about it and starting writing. But all I had really wanted to do was find him again. And now, here he was!

"You're a grown man!" I exclaimed, feeling silly as soon as I said it.

"Do you prefer the child?" Daniel asked. Before I could answer, his body shifted its shape and became the familiar form of the seven-year-old. Sparkling, clear blue eyes met mine. As I stared at him, he changed back into the tall man.

"Daniel," I sputtered. "Does this have to be like the last time? I mean, do you have to shock me all the time? Can't we do this differently?"

"Do what?" he asked innocently, his eyes crinkling with a smile.

"Well," I stumbled over my words, "I guess I assumed you've come to teach me again." Seeing he was only going to continue to grin at me, I took a deep breath and added, "So what's with the homeless thing?"

"Did you like my metaphor?" he asked brightly.

"What?" I replied lamely. "What metaphor?"

"Well, the trash bin...don't you get it?" He asked, sounding surprised.

"No, I'm sorry. I don't get it." I felt slightly embarrassed and hoped I wasn't flunking one of my spiritual lessons again.

"The trash bin...a person has to move through the trash contained in the personality to get to spirit! Even if it's ugly, even if you are thoroughly repulsed by it, even if you would rather just avoid all the old stuff and walk past it, there's no other way. You just have to dive in and move through it. Pretty good, don't you think?"

"Well, yes. It's very good, actually," I replied. He was right; once we decided we were ready to reach for spirit, we all wanted to just dispense with the refuse of our lives and automatically get there. We wanted to find a specific prayer, or crystal or power spot, something that would catapult us up to where we wanted to be.

That was the paradox, really. If we were really honest about it, that method could only cover over what was kept inside. "Bliss out" strategies would only lead us to a cul-de-sac on our spiritual quest. There we'd stay, more comfortable, perhaps, but not really any closer to finding spirit.

I knew a lot of people like that. Once they found their method, nothing could budge them. For years, they would stay with a particular form of meditation or practice, feeling great, even feeling high. But I remembered reading a text in Buddhist philosophy that now made sense to me. It talked about that feeling of bliss as really being one of the roadblocks on the spiritual path. You ran the risk of never going any farther. Sure, it felt a lot better there than most of the places you'd been, but it wasn't your true destination.

"You've got it, Karen," Daniel said, clearly showing me he had not lost his capacity to simply read my mind.

"I still can't do that." I said, frustration powering my words.

"What?" he replied innocently.

"You know perfectly well what. I want to be able to read someone else's mind like you do. When can I learn how to do that?"

"In time," he said without elaboration.

"Where are we?" I said, following him like an innocent puppy. I had no choice with Daniel; I had learned that lesson very well in the last round with him. Whatever he decided to show me, I might as well relax into gratitude and let it happen.

"Well, what does it feel like?" he asked quietly, continuing to travel.

"It feels wonderful! So protected, warm, loving, and soft." I answered, accepting the luscious sensations. A silly grin crossed my face. "It makes me wish I could stay here all the time!"

"Well, there are other places we need to go. But I thought I'd start you out slowly," Daniel said cryptically.

"Start me out..." I trailed off. "Daniel, could we establish some ground rules here?" I said, knowing perfectly well it wasn't going to do me any good.

Laughter followed my pleas, and he answered with a less than comforting statement, "But Karen, those shocking experiences are so good for you!"

He stopped so suddenly, I almost crashed into him. Gesturing, he said with a certain deliberate tone, "Here. Let's do this one."

Then, as was his custom, he disappeared.

Three

"Do this one?" I cried, turning in a circle in a fruitless search for Daniel. "God, I hate it when he does that," I muttered. Squinting through the silver light, I tried to see him. "Daniel! Come on! I know you're here somewhere. Why don't you just come out so I can see you? Besides, I don't know what 'let's do this one,' even means. Do what?"

The light began to swirl and then, coalesced into a spacious hallway that seemed to have no end. On either side, hundreds of doors stretched as far as I could see. "Oh great," I thought, the familiar sinking feeling pulling my heart into my shoes. "This is like one of those scary dreams with all the doors and the monsters behind them. Which one am I supposed to go through?"

But I already knew the answer. One door seemed brighter than the others and now began to throb with a peculiar intensity. Violet light streamed from the small space underneath it. I tried to calm myself by remembering that I had survived everything so far. I might be uncomfortable, even desperately uncomfortable, but I would survive in the end. At least I was fairly sure I would.

Now that I really looked at it, the door didn't seem so dangerous after all. What could happen? Taking an enormous breath, I settled my hand on the shiny knob and turned. With another breath, I pulled up all my courage and pushed it open.

This body was strong! We ran at an incredible rate, straight up the side of a hill. I felt no fatigue, and no sense of being unable to keep up. "Demni," maybe that's who I was!

Four

———

"Go! Go! Go!" The man beside me shouted. I looked at him, too stunned to move. Enormous, muscular, and filthy, his hair flew out from his head like someone who had been struck by lightning. He charged at me, his face fiery with rage.

I tried to step out of his way, but a huge forearm crashed into my back. Stumbling, eyes wide with fright, I scrambled to dodge further blows.

"Get going!" he shrieked. "Demni, what's wrong with you, boy?" A mud-caked boot flew out to kick me.

I had no idea where I was; the barren hillside offered no clues. "Demni?" I choked. "Who's Demni?"

Intensely frustrated, the man glared at me. Suddenly, he turned toward a sound in the distance. "Come, boy. Come!" he commanded, pulling me by my hair.

"Wait!" I cried. "Wait a minute. Who the hell are you?"

He paid no attention but continued to drag me along. Trying to relieve the painful grip he had on my scalp, I gasped, "All right. All right," and matched his stride.

Glancing at me with a puzzled expression laid over his ferocious face, he began to run faster. There was nothing to do but hurry along with him.

Where was I? There was a steady rain falling over the empty, rolling hills. It must be late in the afternoon; an eerie gloom surrounded everything. As I ran beside him, I felt urgency and fear flow from his body like the blood from an injured animal.

Behind us, there were shouts. Glancing back, I saw five brawny men powering after us. These people were like something from another time. Wait a minute!

I looked down to find a body that was thoroughly unfamiliar to me. Large, male, hairy and muscle-bound, I was covered with grime. A ghastly odor surrounded me—a smell which rose up from this extraordinary body.

Daniel! I called silently, desperate to avoid contact with any more of these creatures. Were the men behind us our enemies or were they friends?

This body was strong! We ran at an incredible rate, straight up the side of a hill. I felt no fatigue, and no sense of being unable to keep up. "Demni," maybe that's who I was!

An odd sort of hide formed my clothes. It seemed to be stripped sheep or goat skin. It was impossible to determine what it was underneath the layers of muck? It was cold here and the covering only extended over my thighs. My arms were so big. Dirt, twigs, and dried blood lay in tangled confusion over the strong muscles.

As I ran alongside the man, his craggy club thumped like a drum beat on his thigh. Tethered to his waist by a long cord, it was a deadly thing. Made of sinew, a rock was attached on the end. Clearly, he was a warrior.

We ran for a long time. The steady rhythm compacted my mind into a peculiar familiarity with this place. My heart began to roar. Soon, it was howling like a creature born of these hills. The man no longer seemed strange. His blood mingled with mine; his anger surged through my being.

I was no longer trying to avoid his wrath. Now, we were two companions in a race for life. They were behind us somewhere. My mind repeated an imperative, go, go, go, go. I gripped the weapon at my side, ready to pull it to battle. The passion to survive crashed in my ears as my powerful legs carried me across the hills that I knew so well.

Sweat cascaded into my eyes. I cast it away with a strong hand which had known many deaths. My mind screamed its passion: no one could be allowed to take our land from us. No one should defile our territory! My breath came harshly now, and pounding rage mixed with the heat pulsing from my body.

At the crest of a hill we had shelter. Genete had seen to it. And the food and water...were they still there after all these months? I saw an opening at the base of the rocks. Barely different from the ground it kept company with, that opening led to shelter burrowed out of the hillside.

Falling to our hands and knees, we crawled into our safe place. The others quickly followed and rushed to pull brush over the doorway.

Genete asked my question, "How far behind are they?"

"Maybe back at the seventh hill," Sonae answered. Somehow, I knew that he was the best man to be with in battle.

"Best to stay here," he continued. "They will pass us, then stop for nightfall. We can go back the other way at first light." I nodded my head in agreement.

"Boy." Again, he had called me "boy." How long would it be before he saw I was a man? How many men must I kill before he would see me as worthy?

"Demni...you in your right head now?" Genete was angry with me, as he should be. My refusal to keep up had been an unforgivable disgrace. I desperately wanted to regain his respect. I stood up as tall as I could and met his intense brown eyes straight on.

Batting his own matted head, Sonae interrupted my answer with an unwanted explanation, "Hit too hard." Why did he always do that? I had been born of his sister, but I had no need for his kindness.

"He'll be all right in a few days," he added, wrapping shame around my heart.

"Demni...food!" Genete growled. Turning, I was inexplicably confused about where to find it.

He stared a long time without blinking and then slowly rose and came toward me. As he advanced, I braced for a well-justified punishment. Instead he reached high over my head and brought a leather packet down from a crevice in the wall. Opening it, he offered the well-rotted wing of a plow bird. I had eaten such things a thousand times. But revulsion surprised me by closing my throat. Shrugging, Genete took my food to the others.

Shivering in the embrace of the cold, we crouched for a long time in the darkness. No one spoke. The only betrayal of silence was the sound of urine reaching the ground in a corner of the shelter. Abruptly, there was a hideous sound outside. Like wild animals crashing through the brush, the howls of many men pierced the walls of the hovel. Instantly, springing to our feet, we pulled our clubs and rocks from their carrying places.

Fury screamed its way through my body and my heart drummed the beat of impending battle. It was only a moment before the six men we had hoped to fool rushed through the doorway.

Mighty as an animal, I bared my teeth and thundered the sound of death. Amid ferocious shrieks and cries we swung madly at one another. There were no rules here. No one would survive. Genete fell and then death announced its presence with blankness in forever-open eyes. Three strangers charged at me; their clubs raised high. The terrible realization that my life was about to end splintered my mind.

Blows crashed down on my head and shoulders, and pain replaced my other senses. Struggling to survive, I crumpled onto my side. Then, I felt the agonizing stab of cold metal. My mind shouted in vain: "Death, death is here!" Flooded with horror and grief, I continued to lash out with my knife. The blood of a stranger spurted across my face. But now...I was finished.

Suddenly, what had been my body was very far away. Caught on an invisible current, I slowly sailed upward toward the roof. The young man's body that had been mine lay silent and mutilated below me. The dark brown eyes were wide and stared up at me.

Gently I traveled, right through the top of the hiding place and into a glorious indigo velvet sky. Already, it was decorated with fragments of silver. I continued to rise straight into the heart of a star and shattered into a thousand pieces. Shooting out the other side, I knew that Demni was forever gone.

Warmth washed me clean, and arms held me close. I was like a small child, wrapped in the arms of love. Limp and welcoming, I simply accepted what was given. I began to let all my memories go.

Five

There was a flute playing somewhere. It made such a sweet sound. Music wrapped its way around my battered being and I silently wondered where it was coming from.

A gentle violet light wafted around me, and I heard the deep notes of a cello. The flute wound itself around a familiar melody, adding a tone of joy.

I continued to float, carried somehow on the music. The light underneath me felt like a gentle benediction. Drifting up and down, rising and falling on the breath of the flute, the cello added strength enough to keep me aloft.

Someone was here. Many were here. I felt the caress of a hand, the brush of fingers, and a whisper in my no-longer ears. I couldn't quite hear what he was saying...but oh, there was such love here.

"Come, come my sweet one...it is time."

Warmth washed me clean, and arms held me close. I was like a small child, wrapped in the arms of love. Limp and welcoming, I simply accepted what was given. I began to let all my memories go. Flashes of violence were immediately removed. The hands were everywhere. They stroked and comforted me from every direction.

"You have done so well. Thank you my dear one. You are loved...you are so very loved."

Murmurs surrounded me. Soft whispers and the fragrance of orange blossoms wrapped around the sound of the flute and cello, now far in the distance.

"Open your eyes. Open your eyes." I didn't want to move but wanted to savor the delicious sensations of hot oiled hands which left nothing unattended. "Open your eyes. It is time to go home."

"Home?" I whispered. "I don't want to go anywhere."

A gentle laugh accompanied a soft touch to my eyelids. "Oh, I know. I promise, you will want to be where we are going."

"Am I dead?" The question rippled through me, but it seemed unimportant.

"Oh dear one, each time you forget. Of course this is death, but there is no death, not really. Surely you remember that?" The voice sounded familiar, and I decided to crack my eyes open just enough to see who he was. Tentatively, my lashes pulling away from my skin, I gained enough space to see.

Joy exploded through my being, and I cried out the only words possible. "Oh...Oh my God."

Six

The most glorious thing I had ever seen, he was made of purest light. His form held undulating waves of palest silver, pink, and gold. His radiant eyes were a clear azure. Deep compassion and fervent love filled his luminous face.

"Who...who are you?" I whispered.

He did not answer but began to sway before me and the waves became spiraled strands of spinning light. Music played again, now rhythmic, slow, and sensuous. The sound invited my heart to dance in a way I knew from somewhere long ago.

Moving toward me, he stroked my body, his touch at once so exciting and so tender. Sliding down my body, his light began to penetrate inside the boundaries of my being, and I responded with something I did not know I had.

He sang to me, not with a voice, but with his heart. My own heart began to rise and vibrate, bringing swells of intense pleasure. The waves rose and fell, each time carrying me higher and higher.

"Thank you," he whispered, now beginning to weave his strands of light throughout my being. "Thank you."

Caressed deep inside, there was nothing for me to say, and nothing for me to do, except match his rhythm with mine.

"You are so loved," he sighed, moving deeper into my heart. "So loved...thank you."

Now in a blissful daze, I did not know what he was thanking me for, but it did not matter. My body had blended with his; my mind had drifted away without a goodbye.

"Come my dear one...come now...it is time."

As his scent enveloped what was left of me, vibrating strands of shimmering silver and gold wound around each other. On and on we went, pulsing, rolling, and swaying. Now we were inseparable, and indistinguishable, only light passionately fused with light. Surges of joy built higher and higher, then broke in a crescendo of ecstasy, and went upward again.

Finally, his rhythm slowed and gradually, we separated from one another. A familiar sadness replaced my joy as I acknowledged his request and offered my devotion.

It was time. I had to return to the Earth.

Seven

The city was silent as dawn crept over the mountains behind Boise. Trembling uncontrollably, I leaned against the cold brick wall of an office building and tried to steady myself. My breath came in short, quivering bursts, and my mind snapped and waffled like a flag in the wind.

There was no one in sight. For that, I was deeply grateful. A jumble of emotions obscured my ability to think clearly, and I didn't want to have to talk to anyone. Several hours had come and gone since Daniel had appeared and invited me into the dumpster.

Into the dumpster! That sounded ridiculous. How could I possibly explain what had happened to me? Of course I hadn't literally spent all this time in the dumpster, but where had I been?

I smiled a little and closed my eyes for a few moments. Delicious memories soothed my heart as I remembered the lover I had found. Who was he? More importantly, how could I find him again?

But right now, all I wanted to do was go home, pull the covers up over my head, and try to convince myself I hadn't gone crazy. A songbird greeted the impending arrival of the sun and unwittingly offered me comfort. Gathering my strength, I aimed myself toward my car, still two blocks up the street.

"Hello, Karen."

The words came so softly, I wasn't sure I had heard anything. Shaking my head in an attempt to clear my confusion, I stopped, turned around, and searched the empty street.

"Karen."

This time I was sure the voice existed outside of my own mind. "Daniel?" I whispered cautiously. "Is that you?"

The touch on my shoulder nearly brought me out of my shoes. "Of course it's me," Daniel said. He stood beside me, the familiar grin on his face.

An empty bus bench offered respite for my quaking nervous system, and I sank gratefully onto its hard surface. Daniel sat down beside me, and I felt his warm body lean slightly into mine.

Pulling up my courage, I asked, "What was all that? What did you just put me through?"

"Just one of your lifetimes," he said quietly. "And one of your deaths."

"Oh my God," I whispered. "That warrior, Demni, that was me? Are you saying I just went through a past life experience?"

"Indeed."

My mind begged me not to ask for more information, but I couldn't help myself. "Death was so different from what I ever would have expected! Who was that man who came to me?"

Daniel laughed and patted my knee. "That was your soul, of course."

"Soul..." I trailed off, hardly able to accept what he had said.

"Soul."

In the silence, the word traveled through me, setting off an uncontrollable shaking. Daniel didn't rescue me. He waited while I struggled with the waves of understanding that threatened to engulf me.

Finally, I stammered, "But...but...my soul was male!"

"The soul is neither male nor female, Karen. It only appears in the form that is most comfortable for you."

"How could Demni and I have the same soul?"

"You have had many lifetimes on the Earth, Karen. Each of those lifetimes was created by the same soul."

"Daniel, nobody would expect an encounter with the soul to be like that!"

Most of us believed that the soul was some esoteric, angelic kind of thing. We thought that it lived someplace far away. If we could only be good enough, we hoped that our soul would accept us and, someday, lead us into heaven. But I already knew better.

In our last series of encounters, Daniel had taken me into the realm of heaven. I had learned that my soul was intimately close. In fact, it surrounded me with its loving energy each moment of my life. My soul wasn't interested in counting how many faults I had. It loved me unconditionally and constantly. But the experience I had just been through had been so passionate, and so erotic! God help me, my soul had been the most incredible lover I could ever have imagined.

Remembering the overwhelming love I had experienced, my heart pounded with desire. "Daniel, take me back to my soul." I said urgently. "Please! Just take me back to him."

"That would be a violation," he said softly.

"Violation!" I exploded. "What does that mean?"

"Free will, Karen. Earth must always be a place of free will. You can make whatever choices you wish. As much as I would like to take all of humanity straight into the arms of the soul, I can't do it."

Struggling to find a way to get what I so desperately wanted, I asked, "Why do we have free will? If it just causes us to be separated from the kind of love I just experienced, why don't you just take free will away from us?"

"If you had no choice, love would mean nothing," Daniel answered. "Someone held captive cannot truly love or be loved."

As much as I didn't want it to, what he said made sense. If we weren't free, we would lose the very thing that made us human. "But Daniel, I want to be with my soul! I'm using my own free will, and I want to go to him. Why can't I do it?"

"You can," he answered softly. "But there's something you must accomplish first."

"What is it?" I asked urgently. "I'll do anything! Just tell me what I have to do!"

Without answering, he vaporized right in front of me. And I was alone when she came.

Eight

"Daniel isn't real, you know." The female voice came from my left side. Shocked that anybody else even knew about my elusive guide, I turned sharply to see who it could be. My mouth dropped open when I saw her. Momentarily stunned, I stared mutely as she continued to talk.

"He isn't. He can't be. Things like him just don't exist. Personally, I think you've gone crazy."

We were no longer on the bus bench but sitting on a patch of grass by the Boise River. I didn't care where we were. The important thing was this woman looked exactly like me.

She sounded like an irritated school principal and gestured adamantly to underscore her point. "You've got to get control of yourself, Karen. What are people going to think? You're a well-educated, professional woman. You're going to destroy yourself with this kind of nonsense. When I think about all I've done to help move you along in this world, it makes me sick to see you unraveling like this. Get a grip!"

"Who are you," I managed to squeak.

"Speak up if you have something to say," she snapped back. But not waiting for me to answer, she went on with her soliloquy. "We have responsibilities. We have an image to protect. I'm not at all pleased with you right now." She paused to take a breath, and I found an opportunity to finally speak.

"Who are you?" I said with what I hoped was a commanding tone of voice.

"For God's sake," she answered angrily. "If you don't know who I am, you're more confused than I thought you were." Glancing around as if she wanted to make sure no one else could hear her, she added, "I don't want you talking about this spiritual nonsense to anybody! Do you understand me?"

In danger of losing my temper, I jumped to my feet. "Look, I don't know who you are. I don't know why you look like me. But I do know you have no right to tell me what to do!"

The woman glared at me and rasped, "You have me to thank for everything you've got. Don't you dare talk to me that way."

I started to walk away, and she grabbed my arm. "Look at you! You're a mess. You're out in public, and your hair isn't even properly combed. What if we run into somebody who knows us? By the way, isn't it about time to go for a makeover? We're getting older. We've got to keep up. If you'd just pay attention, I think we could get away with telling people we're five years younger... what about plastic surgery? It's time to think about these things."

"What the hell are you talking about?" I said, wrenching my arm from her grasp. "I'm not staying here with you, and I'm certainly not going to talk to you anymore!"

"Oh yes you are," she snarled, matching my pace as I walked away. "I'm what makes you. Never forget that. Without me, you'd be nothing. Did you call the dentist for an appointment? We've got to keep those teeth looking good. What about the lawn care people? We don't want to be the only people on the block with a brown lawn this year."

"Why are you doing this?" I asked pleadingly. "Leave me alone."

"What do you mean, 'why am I doing this?' she said, mockingly. "I'm trying to restore order. I can't believe you've gotten yourself involved with this spiritual claptrap. What a terrible waste of time. We have so many things to do; so many people rely on us. I'll not have you spending time on nonsense."

"It's not nonsense!" I retorted. "Daniel is real. I've just been in the arms of my soul. What could possibly be more important than that?"

"Reality. Being sane," she growled. "There is no soul. You can't see it; you can't prove it. It doesn't exist."

"That's not true!" I shouted, desperate to get this annoying person to shut up.

"You tell me what your soul has ever done to get your bills paid," she snapped back.

Like a lightning bolt shooting across a midnight sky, I suddenly understood who this woman was. "You're my social mind!" I roared.

Daniel had taken me face to face with this destructive part of humanity before. The social mind existed inside most people on the Earth, but it wasn't a creation of spirit. Filled with anger, resentment, fear, and insecurity, it knew nothing about the world of spirit. As far as it was concerned, life was restricted to what could be seen, heard, touched, or tasted. Its voice constantly invaded my mind with a litany of concerns. It beat me up emotionally every chance it got. My social mind was an enemy of the soul. In fact, Daniel had said that the social mind was really the Antichrist! Its purpose was to sustain its own existence and never let us hear or see our souls.

Humanity had gotten caught in the grips of its own creation. The social mind held no hope and no love. Once this implant from the outside world cut us off from the energies of spirit, we were forced to try to gain what we needed from the outside world. This led to an ever-present anxiety because we instinctively knew that the social mind was false. After all, no matter what we did in this lifetime, no matter how much we earned or achieved, it all came to an apparently deadly end. After this life, eternity stretched, totally unexplained.

"Social mind, social mind," the woman chanted back at me. "Just more of your fantasies. I'm you, and you know it. I'm what occupies your mind almost every moment of your life. I keep you on track. I make sure you do what you're supposed to. I fill your mind with what's truly important in this life."

"No you don't!" I cried. "You keep me from knowing who I truly am. You fill up my mind with constant chatter so that I never get a chance to hear the voice of my soul. "

"If this soul is so real, why doesn't it just speak louder?" she spat.

"It can't! I have to get you out of the way so that my soul can be heard. It can't shout over you. It won't violate my free will. If I allow you to fill up my mind, it will just wait until I make space for it." Seeing that I wasn't getting anywhere with her, I sighed and tried to be compassionate. "Look, you have no way to understand anything about the soul. It's useless to try to explain it to you. Daniel showed me that you aren't even real!"

"Of course I'm real. I'm your constant companion. I'm what you hear in your own mind. I'm you."

"No you aren't!" I shouted. "I'm much more than you! You're just everything I've learned from the outside world. You're the voice of most of my school teachers, and every other person who was so stuck in their own social mind, they thought it was all there is. You're just a horrible collection of other people's ideas."

"That's ridiculous and you know it."

"No it isn't! You use my energy against me. You punish me from the inside for not doing enough and not being enough. You create pain and misunderstanding wherever you go."

"So," she rasped, "just who do you think you are?"

"You can't understand," I repeated wearily. "Daniel explained that you're only capable of understanding other social minds. The only kind of energy you attract is that of other social minds."

"Kind of energy?" she asked sarcastically. "More spirit-babble."

"Don't tell me you don't know anything about energy!" I commanded. Daniel had shown me that almost everyone on Earth had a social mind. The social minds communicated with one another outside of our conscious awareness. They had the ability to grab energy from each other and use it to build their own power. "You steal other people's energy all day long. Don't deny it. I've seen exactly how you do it!"

"I just take what we need," my social mind answered angrily. "It's a hard world out there. There are takers and the taken. That's reality."

"It's like that because of the social minds!" I replied adamantly. "You can't perceive the love our souls offer us without interruption. You think you have no other source of energy except that which comes from the outside. This ugly world of winners and losers exists because all the social minds make it that way. There isn't really any shortage of what humanity truly needs."

"And what would that be?" my social mind mocked.

"What we need to do is get rid of you, and all the others like you! If we did, we'd all see and hear and know our own souls every moment of our lives. We'd be able to offer each other love, comfort, and joy. There would be no war for energy, because we'd all have more than we could ever possibly use."

"Just who do you think you are, missy?" my social mind shouted indignantly.

"I'm a precious creation of a passionate, beautiful soul," I shouted back. "I'm much, much more than you could ever be. More than you could ever be capable of understanding." Calming myself I added, "I admit that I allow myself to be captured in your little world, but you're not all that I am. My consciousness, my being, is much larger than you."

"That's insane."

"No, it isn't. Daniel showed me who I really am. When I'm stuck in your world, I can't see the beauty around me. I can't see or hear anything of spirit. I can't feel the love that surrounds me. You try to destroy all of my dreams. You fill my mind and my heart with an endless stream of worry and resentment. You make me think that I'm only as worthy as my last accomplishment."

I paused and remembered what Daniel had taught me about the social mind. There was no purpose in arguing with it. If I waited for my social mind to recognize spirit, I would be imprisoned forever.

I closed my eyes and worked hard to detach myself from the judgmental tirade that continued to rain over me. Taking several long, deep breaths, I tried to shift my attention from my mind to the center of my heart.

When I opened my eyes, the angry woman was gone. She had been replaced by something I had never seen before.

Nine

She stood about five feet away from me and held out her arms. Her face was luminous, radiating a gentle glow. "Hello, Karen," she said softly. Her voice was musical, peaceful, and calm.

"Who are you?" I whispered; almost afraid she would disappear as quickly as she had come.

"I am you." She answered with a smile that reflected the dawn. "I am the part of you that was meant to be on the Earth."

I sat mesmerized. Her face was mine, but it was filled with an awesome joy. Slowly, she walked over to me and extended one light-filled hand. Then, she placed that hand directly over my heart, sending waves of happiness through me. "I am with you all the time. It is you who chooses to stay inside your social mind where you cannot see me."

Confused, I asked, "But, you aren't my soul, are you?"

"No," she answered gently. "But I can see our soul every moment we are on the Earth."

"*Our* soul?" How could that be? Daniel had told me that universal law mandated that there could only be one soul for each body.

"I am what Daniel calls your natural mind," she said.

"You're my natural mind?" I gulped and added, "But you're so beautiful!"

"Just as you are meant to be." She sat down in front of me and held my hand in both of hers. "You have already learned that your social mind is a false construction, made of the energy of other social minds. It was never meant to exist"

I took a deep breath. "Daniel told me that I wasn't supposed to be trapped inside my social mind. I had another part of me that my soul created—my natural mind—you!"

"And what did he tell you about me?"

"That you could hear and see my soul all the time. If I broke free of my social mind and went to be with you, then there would be no confusion or fear. I would live as my soul designed me to."

"The way humanity has chosen to live is tragic. The souls send their love and reassurance. They ask only that you open yourselves to them. But you are like little children who have gotten lost in a dark closet. There you cower, afraid and alone. The souls cannot open the closet door. That would be a violation of free will. But they beg you to come out and live in the light of your larger home. They ask you constantly to come to them and receive their love and care."

"We don't even know there's anything else but our closet!"

"That is why Daniel has come to you, Karen. To remind everyone that there is a choice. To unscramble your religious teachings so that you can have again all the information about leaving your confinement and rejoin the love that has always been there for you."

Suddenly anxious, I looked over my shoulder for the angry woman. "Where did my social mind go?"

"Oh," the beautiful woman sighed. "She can return at any time. Once she does, I can only disappear."

I grasped her hand tightly and said, "But I want you to stay! Please don't leave me."

"It is your choice, Karen. Your social mind is cunning, manipulative, and powerful, but ultimately, you decide whether she comes or goes. You have a choice about where to place your consciousness. You can put it in the dark closet of your social mind. Or you can move it into a much bigger place. If you insist on staying in the closet, you will only be able to perceive reality through the eyes of the social mind. Remember, it does not have the capability to see spirit."

A duck floated by on the river, seven babies busy behind her. The woman smiled and extended her hand. As if answering a compelling call, the duck turned and scrambled on shore. Like a swarm of bumblebees, her children followed her out of the water. Amazed, I watched as the ducks climbed into the lap of my natural mind. There they shook themselves off and comfortably began to preen.

"How did you do that?" I gasped.

"It is the presence of spirit they are responding to," my natural mind answered. "They know there is nothing to fear. My heart is completely open and filled with love for them." Very gently, she ushered the flock back into the water.

Suddenly, I heard a humming sound. Like a beautiful lullaby, the song seemed to rise and fall from a thousand places. "What is that?" I asked, looking for the source of the music.

My natural mind laughed softly and said, "Oh Karen, you've been away from me for so long. You really don't know, do you?"

"No, I'm afraid I don't," I said sadly.

"Those are the voices of the trees."

"The trees have voices?"

"Of course they do. Everything sings." She stood up and pulled me to my feet. Then, she walked me over to a tall cottonwood tree. "Listen very carefully," she whispered.

Sure enough, the tree hummed in the increasing sunlight. "Why haven't I heard that before?"

"I'm afraid you have spent a great deal of your lifetime right in the middle of your social mind."

My heart started to tumble with excitement. "Are you telling me I could hear the trees all the time if I decided to leave the closet of my social mind?"

She laughed again. "You are meant to hear all the life around you sing. This is only a surprise to you because you've been captured by your social mind. The ability to see and know everything has always been within you. That ability isn't extraordinary. It's the way you were made!"

Abruptly, I heard a terrible voice. "You've totally lost your mind, you know."

My natural mind had vanished, replaced by the enemy of spirit. This time, I knew exactly who she was. Determined to be free, I glared at my social mind. "Get away from me!" I shouted. "I'm not going to allow you to take over my life anymore!"

"Calm down," she snarled, her lips curling in an ugly display of power. "You can never be free of me."

"Help," I called silently. "Daniel, come and help me with this."

Instantly, I stood in a completely different place.

Ten

An incredible vista had appeared before me. Clearly, I was no longer on the Earth. An enormous plain seemed to extend out into forever. Layers of shimmering, radiant light illuminated this place with the transparent colors of the rainbow. Thousands of sparkling souls occupied the space. Filled with effervescent, shimmering light, they were constructing beautiful forms. Appearing like gossamer grids, these forms were created out of the light from each soul's heart.

Now, one magnificent soul came to greet me. Her eyes filled with limitless love, she said simply, "Hello, Karen."

"I've been here before," I breathed. "These are the souls of humanity."

"Yes, they are," she whispered.

In awe, I followed the soul across the vast expanse, all the while watching the magnificent work of those who lived here. "That energy coming out of them is going to become a life on the Earth, isn't it?"

"Yes," she said softly. "Watch carefully, and you will see exactly how each human being is made."

The light that made her being began to vibrate faster and her heart started to spin. Soon, she began to pull strands of silver and gold from that heart. She took those strands and began to weave a sphere. Soon, a magnificent, multi-chambered structure appeared. She sang as she worked, "Come my cherished being, soon you will go to the Earth."

When the sphere was complete, she filled it with sparkling particles of gentle violet light. They floated, unencumbered all through the structure, and seemed to vibrate in accordance with the energy of the soul. "What is that?" I whispered, afraid to disturb her work.

"Why, this is the heart of the person I am creating," she answered. "The heart is the place where the natural mind will live. It is also the place where I can be heard. As you can see, I have filled this heart with my love. I will continue to try to replenish that love all through the person's lifetime."

"To try?" I trailed off.

"Often," the soul said sadly, "a person leaves his heart and builds a social mind. That social mind can become so strong; it is very difficult for the energies of the soul to find their way in. Spirit can do anything, except violate free will. Many times, people cry that God does not love them. But they stand in a place where God is not allowed to enter."

"In their social mind."

"All good things come through you, and not from you. When you live in your natural mind, spirit can flow through you, and out into the world. Each person must decide whether he or she wants to receive all the gifts of spirit or align with something that is frail and full of fear—something that will disintegrate in its seventh or eighth decade no matter what you do."

"When you put it that way, it's not too hard to choose which way to go!"

"When you go into the natural mind, you enter a place of stillness and receptivity. Time and space dissolve. Your natural mind has no judgment, and it does not need to compete for energy. Compared to your social mind, it is so quiet; it may even appear to be absolutely empty. But sit with your heart open, and ask with all that you are: 'Where is my soul?' Suddenly the silence and emptiness around you will become full of light and love. You will hear an answer, 'I am here,' and you will realize that your soul was there all the time."

"Do not be afraid when you hear your soul speak. Open your heart even more. Call out, 'I am here, too.' Then, you will experience the mystical union of the bride and the bridegroom—of the soul, and the being that it created."

"Let go of your philosophical notions about love in favor of your lover. Leave your concepts and your religious teachings behind. Cast away your technique manuals about making love and move into the bed of your lover. You can know the touch of the one who made you. You can feel the spiritual power which sustains your life."

"That's why so many people talk about a deeply moving experience as being transcendent!" I cried. "When you go into your heart so profoundly, you connect not only with the deepest part of yourself, but you touch your own soul."

"Exactly," she smiled.

Next, she wove a complex form around the spinning heart. Its energy was different somehow. Its vibration was a little slower than that of the heart. As I watched, the soul attached little beads of silver, rose and amber to the threads of golden light. "This will be the nature spirit that belongs to the person I am creating," she answered my unspoken question. "It will build the physical body that the heart will be the center of. These beads contain all of my instructions about the body I wish the person to have. Sometimes, I create a body that is not meant to live a long time on the Earth. Sometimes, I even give instructions that result in a physical body with many limitations. I always create the perfect physical body for the needs of a particular lifetime."

"Why would you want a human being to have a body with deficits?" I asked respectfully.

"Oh, dear one," she said gently. "There are many lessons to be learned on your Earth. Sometimes a perfectly healthy body is an impediment to learning. Some of the best lessons about love, acceptance, and a life connected to spirit come from having a different kind of body. Human beings have yet to learn much about compassion."

"That's certainly true," I said, thinking immediately about how cruel we could be when someone had a physical or mental disability.

"The nature spirit will oversee all the functions of the body so that the person will never have to be concerned with them. He will be very busy making sure that your heart beats, and your blood stays in balance. My goodness, he has millions of things to take care of every moment the body is alive."

I remembered what Daniel had taught me about my nature spirit. "The nature spirit is very simple, isn't it? It takes the directions we give him very literally."

"Indeed."

I continued, "If the nature spirit communicates with the natural mind, it finds happiness and can work to carry out the instructions the soul has given to him. But, if we live in our social minds, he's likely to hear a lot of condemnation." I thought about the constant barrage of criticism my own social mind launched at me. I could hardly get through an hour without it telling me that I was too fat, or too tall, or had too many wrinkles, or wasn't meeting societal standards of beauty.

She added, "The social mind frazzles the nature spirit, and makes it very difficult for him to use energy to fulfill your needs."

Pausing for a moment, she pulled an enormous number of strands of light from the region of her own heart. This energy was brilliant white and seemed to have its own intelligence. As the soul released the strands, they quickly organized themselves into another beautiful form. It was much larger than the heart and the nature spirit. Like an enormous lake supporting a tiny canoe, the new form held the heart and the nature spirit.

"What is that?" I asked, amazed by the size of this new creation.

"Each time I send a life to the Earth, I put a very special part of myself into my creation. Many people call this special part the highest self. "

"Wait a minute! The soul and the highest self are not the same thing?"

"No, "she answered patiently. "The highest self is one of the three spirits that make a human being. The highest self is always the same part of me. No matter how many lifetimes the person has had, he or she has always had the same highest self. That spirit comes from me and goes to the Earth to be with the person all through her life. When death comes, the highest self returns to me, and waits to be sent to the Earth again."

If I had understood this soul correctly, I finally had an explanation for why some people thought they knew bits and pieces of former lifetimes. I wanted to check out my conclusions. "The highest self can remember the experiences and relationships it had on the Earth?"

"It can. I know that the concept of being two and being one at the same time is difficult for human beings to grasp. The highest self is an aspect of the soul, but it retains an independent identity," she explained.

"So, we really don't just disappear into nothingness after we die?" I had been a little worried about that. After all my experiences with Daniel, I knew the soul didn't perish when the physical body ended. But I hadn't been sure if we retained any of our own consciousness.

"Of course not," the soul answered gently. "When you die, the highest self returns to be in the center of my heart. It can remember everything that occurred during each lifetime."

"But what's its purpose? We have a soul. What do we need a highest self for?"

"Most human beings are completely unprepared for the full force of the energies of the soul. The highest self is simply more accessible, and more easily understood. In simple terms, it is what many would call your guiding angel. It offers suggestions about the course of your life that are often heard in dreams or felt as intuition. It creates an energy field around the natural mind and the nature spirit that helps to protect them. It helps the nature spirit have enough energy to complete your work on the Earth."

Before I could ask another question, one glorious soul got up and came to stand before us. Powerful waves of love, and unrestrained joy washed over me. "That's my own soul!" I cried.

A deep throbbing sound reached inside me and drew me forward. Streams of silver, gold and blue light began to surround me. Everything I had ever wanted or dreamed of entered my heart and exploded, multiplying past anything I had ever known on Earth.

Now, exquisitely gentle caresses covered every part of me. My soul began to dismantle my consciousness, until I had nothing left but a passionate desire to unite with him forever. "Oh," I sighed, accepting the fluttering kisses which sought my every corner. Relaxing into the warmth, my heart quietly opened like a beautiful set of doors. In a rush of ecstasy, I lost all sense of separation and became one with my lover.

Eleven

"Please, oh please don't make me leave him again. I want to stay with him forever. Oh God, please don't make me go!"

Sobbing against the warm earth, I was consumed with grief. A small, gentle hand rubbed my back, but the offering of comfort did nothing to assuage my sorrow.

"Karen," a child's voice called softly, "there's so much for you to learn."

"I don't want to know anything!" I screamed. "I just want to go home. Please let me go home." Why did I have to be the one to learn? Why couldn't I just stay with my soul?

"You'll go back," he said, finally snaring my attention.

"I will?" I replied, the words cracking apart with turbulent emotion. Opening my eyes, I found Daniel in his seven-year-old body, quietly waiting for me. Dressed in jeans and a bright green t-shirt, his eyes were filled with amusement.

He grinned over at me. "Hi!"

His infectious smile pulled me out of my grief. I rubbed my eyes and looked around. We seemed to be on the backbone of the world. Beautiful, snow-capped peaks stretched into the distance, and an emerald valley languished far below. I decided not to bother to ask where on Earth we might be, and asked, "How come you're a kid again?"

A wonderful giggle came from deep inside his chest. "I thought it might help you lighten up." He looked so merry, so comfortable with himself. "Gosh, Karen," he continued, "you have to remember to keep your sense of humor, or you'll never get anywhere."

I felt a wave of self-pity. "But Daniel, you know what I've been through today! It's been pretty stressful."

"Why?" he asked innocently.

"What do you mean, 'why'?" I said indignantly. "A person can't just catapult all over the universe without feeling overwhelmed."

"Sure you can," he replied. He watched me sputter for a second and added, "I do it all the time."

My mind flip-flopped as it attempted to find a resting place for what he had said. "I'm not you!" I cried. "I'm just a regular person. By the way, I still don't know exactly what you are."

"It doesn't matter," he answered with a bigger grin. "The important thing is to remember who you are. Then, you can live in all the places you're supposed to, just like me."

"What do you mean by that?" I asked warily. It had been nice to experience Daniel as an adult. The seven-year-old seemed to love to try to drive me crazy.

"You know, you don't have to just live inside your body, all stuck and everything. You can live where your soul does, too."

"But you just made me leave my soul, Daniel!" I cried.

"No I didn't." His eyes locked with mine.

"Yes, you did."

"Didn't."

"Did."

"Didn't."

Frustration took over, and I shouted, "Oh for God's sake! If you didn't, then what the hell am I doing back here? I wanted to stay with my soul forever!"

Daniel leaned very close to my face. His blue eyes were bright and suddenly intensely serious. Speaking very slowly, he said, "The only thing that takes you away from your soul is...your...own...darned...social...mind."

After a second of indignation about his attitude, I started to laugh. Of course he was right. How many times did he have to tell me that before I finally got it? A wonderful sense of hope and determination swelled in my chest as Daniel laughed right along with me.

"That's it, Karen," he said exuberantly. "And you can defeat that thing. I know you can!" Through the cascade of giggles he added, "Come on, I want to show you something that you'll always remember, no matter what."

I immediately choked on my laughter and coughed uncontrollably. I didn't want to go anywhere else. Before I could marshal my speech to protest, he vanished.

Grabbing the ground, I struggled to maintain my balance. Eyes wide with fear, I could see the peaks in the distance begin to undulate, like a mythical serpent. The valley below shifted and swerved like a powerful, deep green river.

Twelve

The earth beneath me began to rumble. A low humming came up from deep inside the mountain. Grabbing the ground, I struggled to maintain my balance. Eyes wide with fear, I could see the peaks in the distance begin to undulate, like a mythical serpent. The valley below shifted and swerved like a powerful, deep green river.

"Daniel!" I screamed. "What's happening?"

Laying flat on the ground, I cowered in dread, not knowing what to expect. The earth opened beneath me, and I fell into a quivering hole. Sprays of soil crashed over me, and the humming grew louder. Rocking back and forth, I was dizzy with fear, and the expectation that I would be buried alive.

"Daniel!" There was no word from him, only an escalation of the awesome humming sound. Now the rocking seemed to slow to a gentle, rhythmic motion. An earthquake! My befuddled mind was soothed by the fact that I had a label for the experience. But what was that humming? And shouldn't a quake be over by now? Why had Daniel left me on top of this mountain? Surely, he must have known a quake was about to occur.

I tried to steady my nerves as the rocking motion continued. He had told me again and again that spirit never leaves. I could never be truly alone. "Daniel! I can't see you, but I know you must be here. Help me!"

The humming was now almost deafening. I covered my ears in an attempt to shut it out. Abruptly, I was thrown clear of the hole. Crashing onto my right shoulder, I scooted over the moving earth and finally came to a stop. I looked up to see that I was not alone.

This was Gaia, the spirit who inhabited the Earth! Far from an empty rock hurtling through space, Earth wasn't really a planet. At least not in the way I had always thought it was. Earth was the body of a sentient being from heaven. She had sacrificed herself so that humanity would have a place to accomplish its spiritual growth.

♥

Thirteen

"Excuse me. I'm so sorry," I sputtered, trying to apologize to the two who lay about fifteen feet away from me. Oblivious to my presence, they continued to make love. I backed away from them, stunned that they seemed unaware of the earthquake that continued to make the ground roll beneath my feet.

Looking away from them, I was shocked to find that the mountain had disappeared. The valley was no longer in the distance. There was nothing at all to see, except for the two before me. The humming sound was coming from them.

The woman was astonishing in her beauty. Hers was not a body of flesh and bone but of mountains, oceans, trees, and rivers. Her eyes glowed like the deepest blue sea, and her hair shimmered with a thousand incandescent leaves. Her hands were the intertwined limbs of majestic trees. A glorious, luminous amber, her body was made of gently rolling hills.

This was Gaia, the spirit who inhabited the Earth! Far from an empty rock hurtling through space, Earth wasn't really a planet. At least not in the way I had always thought it was. Earth was the body of a sentient being from heaven. She had sacrificed herself so that humanity would have a place to accomplish its spiritual growth.

But who was the man? Brilliant light burst from his heart. His body was made up of a thousand different animals. His head was like that of an eagle, but astonishing yellow, blue, and green feathers sprang out from the top of it. His eyes were like those of a lion. As I watched, his body continually shifted its form. His limbs now appeared to be those of a great ape, then a strong, black horse.

Gaia and her lover moved in and out of one another, in a glorious, ecstatic dance of love. I was no longer embarrassed. Clearly, this was something I was meant to see. After a long, lingering kiss, Gaia backed away from her lover, and he began to release a low, lingering rumble. Now he spun faster and faster until he finally dissolved in a burst of staggering light. Sparks of gold, blue, cinnamon, and green flew past me at an astonishing speed. His sound diminished and then, he appeared again. Now calm and still, he knelt before his beloved and opened his hands. There, carefully cupped within them, he revealed a tiny bird, covered with brilliant white feathers.

Gaia smiled, revealing a radiant expanse as wide as the sky. The man brought his hands slowly to his lips. A wondrous, delightful chuckle came from deep within him, and the bird began to move. Gaia reached out one luminous hand, and the little bird went into it. She lifted it up and blew one soft breath. The bird flapped new wings and soared away, soon out of sight.

Creation? Could it be that Gaia and her lover had just created a new form of life, right before my eyes? There weren't any new forms of life on Earth. In fact, humanity had canceled out thousands of species in my own lifetime. Without regard for anyone but ourselves, we had destroyed so many environmental systems, that we were at risk ourselves.

Continuing to gaze at the pair of lovers, tears rolled down my face, and my mind struggled to comprehend what I had seen. Suddenly, a powerful wind came from nowhere, and in a sudden blaze of awesome light, they disappeared.

Fourteen

"He doesn't do it very much anymore." I heard Daniel's little voice inside my head. Looking around, he was nowhere in sight. Everything had returned to an ordinary state, and I was back on the mountaintop.

"Come out, Daniel." I said urgently. "I have to understand what I just saw. It was so beautiful, so astounding. I have a million questions!"

"You always do," he answered. His laughter filled the air around me.

"Well, of course I do," I replied, a little petulantly. Surely, he didn't expect me to accept the miraculous without a few questions. "What are you so amused about?"

"Oh, Karen," he said, his child-body materializing right in front of me. A grin still occupied his face. "Sometimes it's amazing to me that you don't already know what's so obvious. The only thing I can do is laugh."

"It's not obvious to me," I answered, my feelings a little hurt.

"Oh, I know, I know," he replied, compassion finding its way back into his voice. "You're like someone who's been hiding in a bunker under the ground. You don't know what's happening up in the real world. That's my job—to show you the real world."

A line from Shakespeare rang in my head. "Dear Horatio, there are more things in the universe than are dreamt of in your philosophy." It had been said perfectly. While we insisted on remaining in the world of intellectual concepts, the universe continued on, waiting for us to acknowledge it.

"You know," Daniel continued, "the amazing thing is, when you see what's really important, you always think something's gone wrong with your mind."

"Right now, it feels that way," I muttered.

"Did you ever consider the idea that your mind has been in the way all along? When you catch a glimpse of spiritual reality, it's a wonderful chance to recognize that."

Holding my head in my hands, I asked, "What did I see back there?"

"Gaia and her lover. You already figured that out."

"But Daniel, I only found out a few months ago that Gaia existed. Now you're telling me she has a lover?"

"Of course." He paused a minute and said, "Who did you think created all the animals?"

My mind had gridlocked. "I don't know."

"Gaia's lover, silly," he said giggling. "Many cultures acknowledge the Creator."

I wondered why he was changing the subject, but replied, "Of course we do. That's God, right?"

"No."

I had a distinct sensation in my mind. More of my beliefs were slipping like burnt cookies off a baking sheet straight into the trash can. I managed to croak, "God and the Creator are not the same thing?"

"No." The grin widened on Daniel's face as he sat and watched me struggle. "And you don't pay any attention to the Creator...at least, most of you don't."

"Daniel," I croaked. "If the Creator isn't God, who is he?"

Fifteen

"When Gaia came from heaven to provide a place for humanity to grow, she didn't come by herself."

Stumbling over my words, I decided to voice only two. "She didn't?"

"No," he spoke slowly. "She came with another being from heaven—the Creator."

"Wait, are you telling me that the Creator isn't God, its Gaia's lover?"

"Yep. Gaia's lover is pure spirit—he animates all the animals."

I swallowed hard. "All the animals belong to one spirit?"

"Uh huh," he said casually. "Their bodies all belong to one soul."

"Holy cow!" I blurted, dissolving into laughter when I realized the truth of what I had said. "But they eat each other!"

"When animals do that, there's a free flow of energy in and out of the body of Gaia's lover. It's like your own blood flowing from your heart down into your feet and back again. The blood doesn't belong to the heart or feet. It's shared by the whole body."

"So, when we kill an animal, we're taking a part of the body of Gaia's lover away from its rightful owner?"

His words came without judgment, "You are."

"And what about evolution? Most of us are convinced we've evolved from the animals."

He smiled sadly and said, "The body of an animal is a joyful expression of Gaia's lover. It's already complete. Never think you grew out of the animals. That's a terrible insult to the animals."

I had thousands of questions. "Wait a minute. You said he doesn't do that much anymore. What did you mean?"

"Although the Creator's still making new forms of life, it doesn't happen very often. I'll explain why in a little while."

I felt my stomach flip-flop at the confirmation that what I had just seen was an act of creation. "Where are these new forms of life? Why don't our scientists know about them?"

"They do know about some of them. The rest are hidden from human beings." He paused a moment and added, "The scientists say the new ones are just a result of mutations of the old ones. They explain them away with something that they think they know."

"We have a habit of doing that," I said sadly. "We like to put things into categories we already have."

"That's right," Daniel said softly. "You do the same thing when you encounter spirit. You decide you have a mental illness, or a brain disease, or something else you think you know about. When you see spirit, and when you encounter a new form of life, it would be much more helpful if you'd allow your old ideas to crumble. Instead, you think your experiences into extinction. Why not take a look at your mistaken idea that you already know everything?"

I was beginning to be certain that we didn't know much about anything. As I tried to choose one question from the jumble in my mind, he grinned and said, "Come on. It's time to go back and experience another one of your lifetimes."

My heart immediately began to pound, and everything went black.

Sixteen

The dust rose in soft, billowing froths as I ran toward the sacred mountain. They were red with the body of Mother Earth and my mouth was parched with the need for water, but I continued steadily toward the east. Already, my grandfather had begun to leave the sky. Dipping down toward his other world, he would soon be out of view. I had to hurry.

I was only a boy. Eleven winters was hardly an honorable achievement. But I had such love for grandmother and grandfather. Even now, tears threatened to find their way onto my face. I could not allow such a thing. It was only for children and women. If I could not show my worthiness, I would not be blessed.

It was a special day—the fifteenth day of the moon. Today, it was possible to see grandmother and grandfather at the same time. Many moons had gone by with too many clouds in the sky. It had been such a long time since I had seen them both at once.

I chastised myself for not leaving the village sooner. But there had been preparations to make. I had to cleanse myself in the river and tie my hair with the feathers of an eagle. My arms had to be painted with the faces of grandfather and grandmother so that they would know I had come to honor them.

Scrambling frantically, I reached the top of mountain. From this place, I could see all the horizons. I made homage to the four corners of the world and sat down. I tried to calm my heart, but it was still busy with the run, and too excited at what was to come. Taking the dried corn from its pouch, I made the pathway for grandmother and grandfather to find me. Sprinkling the kernels in a line directly toward my heart, I hoped they would see that I was worthy of their visit.

I carefully shifted my shoulders so that the symbol of grandmother faced directly east and grandfather west. Waiting there, I could hardly breathe. Excitement scurried through my body, and my hands trembled. All around me, hundreds of voices sang. They called into the sky for their Maker. The birds were closest to Grandfather, for they knew how to fly toward his heart. But the deer that rustled in the brush knew his love. So did the humble porcupine that hurried past my legs. Even the buzzing bee that tried to make rest in my hair never forgot who had sent him into the world we shared together.

Suddenly, it was absolutely silent. And there! There she was! Revealing herself over the eastern horizon, grandmother moon entered into this world. Her face was illuminated with the light of her husband. Now in the west, grandfather sun did not depart but waited to bid her welcome. Their union sent a glorious shower of transparent red, purple, orange, and yellow over the sacred mountain. Following the path of the corn, their light swept straight into the center of my heart.

I lifted my face to meet them. Grandmother moon continually showed me that her body was like mine. Each month, she would rise to fullness, and then steadily decline into nothingness. I would grow to be a man, my body full and strong. But I would steadily fade and become old. After many winters, my body would die away.

Grandfather sun showed me that all life was, in truth, eternal. His body never diminished. His life was always in a state of absolute fullness. His radiance pulsed within every living creature. He had created all the animals, sung life into them, and drew that life away from them. But he never ended, and life never ended. It only came and went to live in one place or another.

I could see in grandmother and grandfather the truth of my being. I would have a temporary sojourn in this body that now rested in the arms of Mother Earth. Then, I would be released to

rejoin the All That Is. In time, I would come to be in a body again…
and leave again…and come back again. Each time, Mother Earth
would be happy to see me. And when it was time, she would be
excited to return me home. So, it had always been.

It was time to make ceremony in remembrance of the gifts
grandmother and grandfather had given to me. I sliced open my
skin, and my blood dripped over the earth. This was an acknowl-
edgment that someday, my body would return to the Earth from
which it had come. Then, I blew a soft breath over the blood. This
honored the spirit that was contained in my body—a body that
was nothing by itself.

I stood and raised my arms up high into the air. I released one
long howl of gratitude. Then, bathed in a last burst of blessed light,
I watched as grandfather disappeared. And left grandmother to
reign over the night.

This was Gaia, the spirit who inhabited the Earth! Far from an empty rock hurtling through space, Earth wasn't really a planet. At least not in the way I had always thought it was. Earth was the body of a sentient being from heaven. She had sacrificed herself so that humanity would have a place to accomplish its spiritual growth.

♥

Seventeen

"That's what it means to acknowledge the Creator." Rousing myself from the spell of my experience, I looked over to find the adult Daniel sitting beside me. Back in my familiar body, I was no longer on the sacred mountain. We were now on a bluff, overlooking the sea. Pine trees sent their soothing fragrance over us, and the sun blazed in its approach toward sunset.

I didn't want to talk at the moment, but I noticed something spectacular. As the sun dipped toward the horizon, the light that had played over the water condensed into a narrow band. A brilliant pathway of gold now sparkled from the shore into the horizon. If I were able to actually walk on that path, it appeared as though I would go straight into the orb of the sun.

"Good, Karen. You're seeing it. Keep watching."

As the minutes went by, the pathway shortened like a long carpet being rolled up into the sun. Then, the sun began to disappear into the horizon. As it did, miraculous colors shot across the sky in a dazzling display of orange, red, and lavender.

"Where have you seen those colors before?" Daniel asked gently.

"The fragments of light which spun out of my soul were just like that," I whispered. What was he trying to tell me?

"You see, the sun exists to remind you of your true home. Its brilliant, constant light is like that in heaven. Your physical eyes can barely look at it; that kind of light is too extraordinary to be comprehended by the senses.

"Each day, the sun gives way to the glorious colors of your soul. You can't return home, except by way of the soul. Each of you is given a beautiful pathway that goes right over all the obstacles that seem insurmountable. But, if you follow the path, you will find your way home."

The colors had diminished as night approached. Now an indigo blue, the sky was beginning to fill with stars. "Daniel, is that path of light there every day? I've never noticed it before."

"Of course it is," he said chuckling. "You haven't noticed it, just like you haven't noticed all the other clues."

"Clues?"

"Oh, Karen. Nothing around you is here by chance. Every part of nature was intentionally created to serve one purpose."

My mind rolled to one side. "What purpose?"

"To help you to remember who it is you truly are." He watched me for a moment and then continued. "There are no accidents. Gaia created her body, and the Creator made all living forms so that you'd have constant reminders about how to make your way home."

"Nature is meant to serve as an example to man?" I shook my head and tried to absorb what he was saying. "But doesn't the Bible tell us that man is supposed to have dominion over the animals?"

"That passage was meant to read, 'All life is created as a reminder to you so that you will remember who you really are.' Remember and dominion have the same roots in the language of your Bible."

I was momentarily overwhelmed by the enormity of what he was saying. "Are you telling me that everything was put here to help us return to our souls?"

"That's right," he replied. "Everything of nature was intended to be a mirror of your own spiritual development."

I whispered, "That's what you meant when you said, the clues are all around us."

Daniel looked at me, his eyes filled with unending compassion. "We didn't send you to the Earth alone. You've never been abandoned or forgotten. If you only open your eyes and your heart, you'll see that you're surrounded by millions of teachers."

With that he waved his hand, and everything changed.

Eighteen

We stood in a rushing river of spectacular energy. My body had been left behind, and particles of gold and silver light seemed to speed right through me. They came from a source I could not determine. Yet, I somehow knew there was no end to this powerful torrent.

"Where are we?" I cried.

"In the middle of reality," Daniel answered. I could barely make out his form. It melted in and out of the river, now appearing almost human, and then allowing itself to dissolve and float away from me.

"Reality? This doesn't look anything like what I would call reality!"

"But Karen, that's the whole point. What you determine to be reality is only an illusion."

This place was filled with joy, but I had no idea what he was talking about. Before I could ask a question, he continued, "What you call reality is something decided upon by your mind. In fact, it doesn't exist."

"Of course it exists!" I protested. "I don't understand what you mean."

"Your brain tells you that things exist. But the brain can't see beyond itself. It's only an organ that excludes information and focuses your attention in a certain way. The brain doesn't create your consciousness, it limits it. Here, just look."

Suddenly, the fragments of light seemed to launch themselves out of the rest of the flow. They began to spin around each other and gradually, a beautiful tree appeared.

"Daniel, what's a tree doing in here...out here..." I stammered.

"There is no out, and there is no in. The tree is here because it's a manifestation of energy. The same energy that creates everything you see. But it has no independent existence. Just watch."

Soon, the tree seemed to let its form go. It was swept back into the stream of energy, no longer any different from the other particles of light.

Daniel continued, "Your brain tells you that the tree is a separate, concrete object. But it can't be separate. Nothing can ever be truly separate."

"It can't?

"Of course not. Your brain causes you to solidify the energy. It slows everything down so that it appears solid and permanent. But that tree never existed, and it always existed...depending on how you know how to look."

I felt dizzy and managed to say only two words. "I'm lost."

"The tree is a concept imposed on the energy by your brain. Soon, you can't see anything except your own concepts. But that doesn't change reality."

"But Daniel, how can I know what's real and what isn't?"

"Nothing is real, and everything is real," he answered. "If you learn how to release your ideas about reality, and let the true nature of things come through, you'll see that everything exists only as a manifestation of the divine. It has no true identity of its own."

The energy around me began to swirl and coalesce into another form. Soon, a beautiful orange butterfly appeared and began to fly around me. Profoundly confused, I decided to simply watch it. It wasn't long before the butterfly dissolved back into the energy from which it had risen. Before I had a chance to ask another question, countless animals, plants, insects, and fish appeared and disappeared. Every time I decided that something was truly permanent and real, it melted into the flowing energy.

After some time, Daniel spoke again. "You see, things that seem independently real are only apparitions in the field of space and time. Space and time are functions of the physical brain. Everything always belongs to the whole. It always returns to that whole."

"Everything?"

"You are standing in the midst of divine energy. That energy has caused the Earth, sun, and moon to appear. Your galaxy is a manifestation of divine energy. So are all the forms of life that surround you."

I wasn't sure I had heard him correctly. Stunned, I managed to ask, "Are you telling me that our entire galaxy is only a temporary apparition?"

Daniel smiled and stretched his arms up to the sky. "What seems to you to be a vast and mysterious universe is really an extraordinary cloud of energy directed by Gaia and her lover."

I struggled to put the pieces together. "It's all here to remind us of who we really are?"

"Humanity exists within a special school filled with millions of teachers. Here, look at the humble spider." Daniel reached into the flow of energy, and brought forth the tiny insect, still surrounded by its shimmering web. "It shows you that your body is only a tiny thing which exists within the field of your soul's energy."

He released the spider, and it dissolved into the energy. "Look at the snake." As I watched, a reptile emerged from the light and then, shed its skin. "It tells you that the body is only a temporary covering. It can be left behind without consequence to the true being which exists inside that body."

"And here is what your scientists call DNA." In Daniel's hands, I saw spiraled strands with tiny, shimmering spots attached to them. "This reminds you of the way your soul spun your lifetime from his own energy. What you call genes are there so that you remember how your soul put the instructions for your lifetime onto the strands that make up your energy form."

In awe, I watched Daniel pull a fiery orb from the stream. Before I had a chance to gasp, he repeated what I already knew. "Your sun exists to remind you of upper heaven. Its brilliant light is like that of your true home."

Now he held what I recognized as a giant sequoia in the palm of his hand. "See how your trees and plants all reach for the sun? They live on the energy from that sun, just as you must live from the energies of spirit. Without the sun, the plants can't sustain themselves. They remind you that, without spirit, you cannot exist."

Daniel laughed as he pulled a moose from the stream. "There are so many wonderful teachers! The mammals demonstrate the concept of free will. The mother animal creates her young inside her body, just as your soul created you from its body. Then, she lets them go to find their own way, just as your soul releases you to do as you choose.

"There are clues everywhere!" he said gleefully. "Just look into the eyes of your devoted cat or dog. Find there wonderful examples of unconditional love and uncompromised acceptance— small reminders of the love your soul has for you."

Turning toward me, Daniel's blue eyes were shining with pure joy. He whispered, "One day, even your scientists will see that the face of the divine is reflected perfectly in every cell and atom of all that is."

Then, he began to sing a wonderful series of cascading notes. The river of energy murmured with the voices of a million animals and then began to send up the same notes. Together, Daniel and the energy created a glorious song.

The same song I had heard from my own soul.

Nineteen

Suddenly, I was back on the bluff by the sea. Night had come, and the stars glittered overhead. Daniel was nowhere to be seen. My tears came fast and heavy with the realization that we had never been alone. We had created our own sense of despair by cutting ourselves off from every aspect of spirit. Not only had we lost the knowledge that our soul surrounded us every second of our lives, but we had also blinded ourselves to our teachers on the Earth.

I thought about how many times I had sat inside my house and watched television, while the sunset offered a glorious reminder of my true home. So many times, I had heard people talk about animals as though they were stupid and impossibly limited. But nature wasn't beneath us. We had removed ourselves from its embrace. By doing that, we'd lost the mirror we needed to accomplish our own spiritual growth.

No wonder many of us had been drawn to the words of Chief Seattle. He managed to call us back into remembering what our surroundings were all about. Written in 1855, his message held magic:

"Man did not weave the web of life; he is merely a strand in it. Whatever he does to the web he does to himself. Every part of this earth is sacred to my people. Every shining pine needle, every sandy shore, every mist in the dark woods, every meadow, every humming insect. All are holy."

I lifted my head to gaze upon a thousand stars and realized how incredibly arrogant we had been. We had killed the moon when we landed on its surface and announced that it was only rock and dust. We were killing our universe by measuring and numbering the planets and the stars. We had sucked the meaning out of everything and then believed it had always been dead. It was possible to tear apart even the most miraculous of things with the weapons of the social mind.

Chief Seattle had said, "What will happen when the secret corners of the forest are heavy with the scent of many men and the view of the ripe hills is blotted by talking wires? And what is it to say goodbye to the swift pony? The end of living and the beginning of survival."

Humanity had entered the realm of survival in this century. There was only one thing that could come next. A soft, glowing mist of violet light announced Daniel's arrival before he spoke. "Hello, Karen," he said before materializing into his adult form.

I asked wistfully, "Why does ordinary life seem so different? Why can't I see reality all the time?"

"You've lost your ability to see because you insist on worshipping your brain, the physical senses, and your social mind. If they can't perceive something, you decide that it must not exist. But reality isn't affected by your ability to see or not see. It continues as it is, despite your stubbornness."

I didn't want to be trapped anymore. The beauty of what I had seen called me to action. "Tell me, Daniel," I said urgently. "Tell me how I can be free!"

Twenty

By now, it was so dark I didn't notice that we were no longer in the same place. But when the sun peeked over the horizon, I was amazed to see that our surroundings were very different. Daniel and I sat beside a narrow, dusty road. A line of telephone poles marched into the distance as far as I could see. Huge stone monuments lurched out of the flat, desert floor, and giant cacti sent their green fingers up toward the sky. I decided we had to be in the American Southwest.

The scent of sagebrush reminded me of Boise, and I stood up to stretch. When I turned around, Daniel was gone. "Great," I muttered a little irritably. "Now what am I supposed to do?" At least he had left me on the Earth, and vaguely close to Idaho. If need be, I supposed I could hitchhike my way to the nearest town, call my husband, and get a bus ticket to Boise.

I smiled as I thought of something Gertrude Stein had said, "Everything's so dangerous that nothing's really frightening anymore." Certainly, that was an important thing to remember as far as Daniel was concerned. I pulled up my determination and decided to walk down the road toward the east.

Still cool from its journey through the night, the desert was beautiful. As the sun climbed into the sky, glorious pink light enlivened the barren landscape. Glad to be wearing comfortable shoes, I found a rubber band in my pocket and tied my hair up into a ponytail. I cast my coat aside, smiling a little as I remembered how much I had needed it the night Daniel had reappeared to me. I wondered how long it would be before he made contact with me again.

"I wonder if anybody ever comes down this road." After an

hour of walking, I had spoken aloud, even though there was no one to listen. Every so often, a small animal rustled through the brush, and hawks flew overhead, but there was no sign of human life.

"Need a ride?"

Completely surprised, I jumped and turned around. An old woman leaned out of the window of her ancient pickup, a friendly smile on her face.

"I didn't hear you coming!"

"No, I don't suppose you did," she replied, reaching up to correct the pitch of her battered straw hat. "Bet you're glad I came along, though."

"Yes," I answered enthusiastically. "Very glad. I'm Karen." I reached out to shake her already extended hand.

"Jessie," she replied. "Come on, I'll give you a lift."

I climbed into the weathered green truck and looked more carefully at Jessie's brown face. Her eyes were a lively blue, but they were hard to see among the deep wrinkles that indicated a lifetime of smiles. Her hands were callused and scarred. I thought perhaps she had a ranch out here.

"What's the nearest town?" I asked, peering through the dusty windshield. I faintly hoped I would recognize the name. I certainly didn't want to admit that I had no idea what state we were in.

"Billford," she answered. Motioning toward the floor, she added, "There's water in that canteen. Nothing fancy like you're probably used to, but water nonetheless."

Grateful to soothe my parched throat, I took a long swig, leaned back into the seat, and released a long sigh.

"Oh you're tired, aren't you?" she said, patting my knee. "My place is just up ahead. Would you like to stop for a while? I'll fix you something to eat and you can wash up."

Suddenly overwhelmed with fatigue, I nodded my agreement. After everything I had been through, a few hours' delay in returning to Boise couldn't hurt anything. "How long have you lived out here?"

"A long, long time," she answered. "But now, I can't spend as much time here as I'd like to. As they say, got places to go and people to see." We turned onto a rough road and bounced along for a few miles. Then, she stopped alongside a path that diverted to the right.

"Got to walk from here. I don't like machines too near my house. Come on. It's not far, at all."

Starkly different from the desert surrounding it, I was startled when we made it to her home. Bright white paint covered the clapboard, and neat blue shutters framed the open windows. Lace curtains fluttered in the breeze. Encircled by a picket fence smothered with bright pink climbing roses, the house was small and welcoming. A single towering oak tree provided prolific shade. "My goodness. This is beautiful!"

"I try to keep it up," she said proudly. "Come in. I'll make some lemonade." Jessie took off her hat as we went through the door. I was surprised to see shimmering black hair fall past her waist. She motioned toward the bathroom, and I went in to clean up. I could hear her singing in the kitchen as I splashed water over my face.

When I returned, she led me to a plump, comfortable chair. She handed over the lemonade and a plate filled with fragrantly seasoned beans, vegetables, and potatoes. After I had eaten, an enormous orange cat made his way into my lap. Soon, he was purring loudly and stretching contentedly in my arms. Taking his cue, my eyes grew heavy, and I drifted toward sleep.

"That's right." I heard Jessie say. "When you're all rested, we'll get started."

"Get started doing what?" I murmured peacefully.

"Oh, dear girl," she answered gently. "You have so much to learn."

I should have known better. Daniel had never taken me anywhere without a reason. He wouldn't have left me out in the desert and assumed somebody would arrive to rescue me! Peering over at the old woman, I ventured an obvious question, "Daniel? Is that you?"

Twenty One

Climbing out of my dreams, I cracked one eye, stretched, and remembered where I was. "Hello," I called. Not receiving any answer, I stumbled toward the bathroom. A new toothbrush had been laid out for me, along with a hairbrush and a bright blue ribbon. I smiled, and silently thanked Jessie for her sensitivity to my needs.

Walking out onto the porch, I saw that the sun was very low in the sky. I had slept for hours. "Hello!" I called again.

"Well, hello there," Jessie replied. She came around a corner of the house, a basket filled with roses over her arm. "You had a good rest."

"I'm so sorry," I said sheepishly. "I didn't mean to inconvenience you."

She answered with a smile, "That's perfectly all right. It's nice to have some company."

"I guess I'd better be on my way."

"Yes," she said. "We'd better get started."

Suddenly I remembered she had told me that as I drifted into sleep. What else had she said? Before I had a chance to recapture her words, she added, "You have so much to learn."

I stared at her with my mouth ajar. "Jessie, just who are you?"

"Another teacher," she replied happily. "My goodness, you didn't think you got here by accident, did you?"

I should have known better. Daniel had never taken me anywhere without a reason. He wouldn't have left me out in the desert and assumed somebody would arrive to rescue me! Peering over at the old woman, I ventured an obvious question, "Daniel? Is that you?"

"Oh, my gracious, no!" Jessie laughed. "Come on," she said, disappearing around the corner of her house. I followed her trustingly but came to an abrupt halt at the sight before me.

My knees began to quake like the leaves on an aspen tree. I tried to speak, but I sounded like the croaking of a frog.

"Come on," Jessie whispered as she took my hand. "It's time to learn."

Twenty Two

Eight women sat in a large circle around a roaring fire. Although they were all dressed in the same loose white clothing, their faces told me they had gathered from different parts of the world. Black, white, red, yellow, and brown, they were each astoundingly beautiful.

"Who are these people?" I whispered as Jessie led me into the circle.

"They come from places that still have the teachings from the original continent."

Daniel had told me about an enormous continent that had existed in the Pacific Ocean thousands of years ago. It had been the home for the first people who were sent to the Earth by their souls. Eventually, people from this place had scattered all over the world. The fabled Atlantis was one of their colonies. Remarkably accomplished, both spiritually and scientifically, they knew things that we were now only discovering. The continent had ceased to exist, but Daniel had never told me what had happened to it.

Searching the landscape for any sign of transportation, I asked, "How did they get here?"

"True connection with the soul makes many things possible," she answered mysteriously.

"I had no idea that anyone on Earth knew about the original continent. Are you saying that there are cultures that have access to information from that time?"

"Only a few," she answered somberly. "Since the social mind took over your world, it has managed to extinguish the information by annihilating many different cultures. I'm afraid there are a lot of religious leaders who would like nothing better than to stamp out the teaching entirely."

My curiosity was overwhelming. "Where are those places on the Earth?

Her brown face was framed by her long, black hair. She smiled and said," My people came from the original continent."

"Your people?" Understanding blazed through me. "Jessie, are you Native American?"

"I prefer the term First Person," she replied. "We were the first people to arrive in America."

"How did you get here?"

"Some came directly from the original continent by boat. Others went to a different part of the world first and later walked to this region." She watched me carefully and waited for my next question.

I couldn't help myself. "What part of the world?"

"It's now called Tibet."

I swallowed the lump in my throat and needed reconfirmation. "Native Americans...the first people came from Tibet?"

"Some did," she nodded. "But the members of other groups came much later from other places. All the cultures you see represented here share the teaching from the original continent."

Looking around, my attention landed on the striking red-haired woman in the circle. "Where do you come from?

"Ireland," she replied. The lilt in her voice was unmistakable. "My Celtic tradition contains the same information that Jessie's does."

"Oh my God," I whispered, and gratefully sat down beside her.

Jessie grinned and said, "Did you think it was an accident that so many people have become increasingly interested in works about the Tibetans, the Australian Bushmen, the First People of America, the Celts, and the early Hawaiians?"

"I didn't have any idea that the information coming from those different sources was linked somehow!"

"Other places on Earth hold the teaching, as well, but it's kept secret."

"Where?" I pleaded "Where is it kept?"

Jessie paused as if to allow me to gather my mind before she blew it away. "There are many things in the basement of the Vatican which are never discussed and will never be released to humanity."

"So, is humanity being led to rediscover this original teaching?" I asked. "After all, our interest in the lives and beliefs of the cultures you just mentioned was pretty sudden."

"Of course you are," an old woman spoke. As I looked across at her, I realized she must be Tibetan. Her beautiful, peaceful face was Asian. Her smile reminded me of the Dalai Lama.

My heart accelerated. "Who's leading us?"

The woman looked a bit surprised that I didn't put two and two together. "Why, it's all part of the second chance. I know Daniel has spoken to you about that. The Christian era is coming to an end. It's time for a shift of energy—energy that will assist Earth's people to rediscover their hearts."

I had to make sure I understood. "Christianity won't be important anymore?"

"Of course it will," Jessie intervened. "But those who follow the true teaching of Jesus are few in number. Most of what is called Christianity is tragically under the control of the social mind."

Daniel had taught me a lot about that in our first encounters. One only had to look at the lack of knowledge about the natural mind to recognize that Jesus' real message must have gotten horribly mixed up. If it hadn't, our world would be a lot different.

I looked in amazement at the women around me. "You've known everything Daniel has shown me and everything he's taught me, all along, haven't you?"

"Yes," Jessie replied. "But most of the people on Earth have never paid attention to us. In fact, your primary teachers in America, the first people, were nearly exterminated. Now, most of them are isolated on reservations, or have become lost in the social mind themselves. Thankfully, there are a few of us left. However, I have grave concerns about how long we will be able to hear the ancient whispers of our souls."

"It sounds like you're getting the information out just in time!" I cried. "I'm so glad people are beginning to pay attention."

"But now it's your turn, Karen." Jessie said somberly. "If you can free yourself of your own social mind, and write about all you know, many, many people will have a wonderful opportunity to learn."

My heart was heavy with the responsibility Daniel had already given me. Jessie's confirmation of my task was almost overwhelming. I had been an ordinary counselor from Idaho! How in the world could I stand up against a world of social minds?

"Remember," Jessie said quietly. "You don't need to try to convince anyone. Go outside your own doubt and fear, things that are the weapons of your social mind. Simply tell them about what you've seen. Hope they will feel a spark of recognition in their own hearts. If they're willing to do the work, they can flame that little spark. Once ignited, the flame of spirit will burst forth, and burn away the ignorance created by the social mind. That's all."

"That's all!" I cried. "But it's such a responsibility. I've pleaded with Daniel, now I'll beg you—pick somebody else! I'm not strong enough or brave enough."

"That is your social mind at work," the bushwoman responded. "Karen don't thrash wildly and protest in vain. Do your work. Let spirit flow through you, and onto the paper. No one can say what humanity will do with the sacred information that is now coming from many sources. Let go of the outcome and concentrate on allowing the voice of the infinite to be heard through you."

Tears covered my face as I looked around at the gathering of peaceful, powerful women around me. They had courage, and so could I.

"Teach me," I said humbly. "Teach me what I need to know."

Twenty Three

Night had come and scattered her celestial adornment across the blackness. Crimson sparks shot out of the fire, and into the sky. A tall, angular woman climbed to her feet. I held my breath, waiting to hear what she had to say.

"My name is Mariah," she said. "I come from a monastic order living secretly in the hills of Armenia. We have many teachings from the original continent, and we protect the written word that came from Jesus' time. But ours is not the word that has been recorded in the Bible. Those accounts were put on paper by people who were afraid to tell the truth about what they had seen."

"Who wrote what you have?"

"There were many people, both men and women, who had the courage to record what they heard and saw." She laughed ruefully, "They saw that it was useless to try to argue with those who insisted that people couldn't handle the truth about Jesus' teaching. They quietly wrote about their experiences with him and hid the information away."

"Have we ever seen any of their writings?"

"You have small fragments," she said. "They have been found buried in the hills by the Dead Sea. They have been scattered in the writings of the Gnostics."

The woman before me suddenly became unfocused, like a television picture in need of adjustment. I blinked hard, thinking that fatigue had distorted my vision. But she became even more blurred, and to my astonishment, split herself into four pieces. Now, each of those parts became clear and distinct. Her physical body appeared as it had a moment before, but she was surrounded by three bodies made of light. Each shimmered with glorious colors and extended outward in succession.

A translucent cloud of maroon and silver light seemed to cling to her physical body. As I looked closer, that light permeated her body, making it transparent. I could see blood flowing through her arteries and veins. Her organs were perfectly observable, like the anatomical model I had used in college. Suddenly, a voice came out of the cloud and issued a simple request, "What do you wish of me?"

"Who is that?" I whispered, afraid to disturb the phenomenon before me.

"That is my nature spirit," she answered. "I am healthy and strong because my nature spirit takes its direction from my natural mind. It is not subject to the attacks that come from the social mind."

She paused and added, "My nature spirit can do wondrous things. Not only does she take care of all my physical systems, but she is responsible for making the connections between me and other people."

"I don't understand," I said feebly.

"Just watch." The cloud seemed to vibrate more quickly, and a beautiful silver thread came out of it. Gradually, that thread increased its diameter and crept toward me. Afraid, I leaned backward.

"Don't be frightened," Mariah said soothingly. "You're only seeing what goes on all the time between one person and another."

"What is that?"

"It's a hollow cord made from my nature spirit's body. As you can see, its energy is more condensed than that of my other two spiritual bodies. If I concentrate on someone for any period of time, the nature spirit sends out such a cord and attaches it to that person. That's one of the ways that energy flows from one person to another."

As she spoke, the shimmering silver cord made contact with my hand. I was instantly filled with a wonderful sense of peace and acceptance. "Why does it do that?"

"So that we may understand one another without the need for words," she answered. "Without a social mind, I give to you only love and understanding. Unfortunately, the cord will also deliver the contents of an active social mind if the person has not escaped from it."

"So, once a cord is attached, does it stay there forever?"

"It isn't meant to," she replied. "You must understand that your nature spirit does this for you, whether you request it or not. But it will not disconnect unless you tell it to do so. It's very important to sever the ties you have made throughout your day. Otherwise, you will continue to receive the thoughts, feelings, and concerns of everyone you've connected with."

Maybe those cords were responsible for many of my sleepless nights. Often, I couldn't seem to shut off the events of my day, and the emotions they had generated. I had a sudden flash of insight, "Is that how telepathy works?"

"Yes, it is. It is also how close friends and family members can experience a feeling that you're in trouble or need them to call. What is incorrectly called intuition is often simply a message being received along one of the nature spirit's cords."

I thought about all the people in the field of human services who had suffered burnout. Although their hearts were still full of compassion, they had become unable to continue in their professions. They had felt that they were carrying a burden that was too heavy for them to bear. Maybe their nature spirits hadn't severed the cords of energy from all their patients and clients. If that was the case, they were constantly plugged into the pain of those they tried to help.

"Exactly," Mariah said. Seeing my surprise at her ability to read my mind, she nodded toward the cord. "That's how it's done."

Finally, I had the answer to Daniel's ability to read my mind! I grinned and asked, "Can I learn to do that?"

"Of course you can," Jessie said enthusiastically. "It's not a special ability. It's what you were meant to be able to do. Stand up."

I did as I was told, and Jessie whispered, "Just tell your nature spirit what you want it to do. But be very careful to extend your cord from your natural mind. Otherwise, your social mind will grab the opportunity to take over."

I closed my eyes and tried to go into my heart. Silently, I asked my nature spirit to make a connection to Jessie. As I concentrated, a small silver thread emerged from my solar plexus. Astonished, I watched it extend and attach itself to Jessie's heart. A wonderful wave of intense love went through me, and I giggled like a child. "I did it!"

Jessie returned my smile, and I said, "I need to know how to sever the cords my nature spirit makes. There are a lot of people I don't want to stay attached to!"

"You do it with your intent," she replied. "Often, it's helpful to focus that intent on a particular image. You can visualize yourself cutting the cords with scissors, or a knife. Or you can simply concentrate and tell your nature spirit to sever all connections that don't serve your highest good."

I practiced what she told me, and watched the cords connected to Jessie and Mariah simply fall to the ground and disappear. "I thought my nature spirit's ability to run my body was phenomenal, but these cords are really amazing!"

"It does other things, too," Mariah said as she returned to her place in the circle. "But I'll let Maoli show you that."

Twenty Four

"Hello, Karen." The woman who came to stand in front of me was incredibly beautiful. Long, black hair drifted well below her waist, and almond eyes illuminated her gentle, brown face. "I come from what is now called Hawaii."

"I didn't know there was anything left of the old ways in Hawaii," I said sadly. The history of Hawaii was filled with accounts of warfare and missionary intrusion. But somehow, I had known that there was something magical about the people who had lived on the volcanic dots in the middle of the Pacific.

"We have hidden our knowledge," Maoli said. "If we hadn't, it would have been lost forever. Many of Jessie's people have succumbed to the social mind—so it is with my people."

While I mused at the incredible arrogance and power of the social mind, she suddenly said, "Think of something you really want."

I thought for a moment and decided to go with what Daniel had asked me to do. "Okay, I want to write a book about my experiences with Daniel."

All the women in the circle nodded their encouragement. Maoli said, "That's good, Karen. Now, instruct your nature spirit to build an energy form for your book."

"What?"

"Everything that exists began with an idea in someone's mind. If you focus on that idea, and ask your nature spirit for its assistance, it will create what you want on an energy level. That's the very first step toward bringing the idea into reality."

"Wow," I exclaimed. "So, all that stuff about visualization is actually true?"

"The trouble with visualization is that the instruction usually comes from the social mind. It sends down so many contradictory messages the poor nature spirit can't figure out what to do with them all. It starts storing the messages instead of acting on them. When it receives enough messages that are consistent with one another, then it will act. Unfortunately, the only messages that the social mind issues consistently are those that are destructive, demoralizing, critical, and demeaning."

"Go into your heart, Karen, and concentrate on your desire to produce Daniel's book." I did as I was told and was astounded to see a beautiful, rectangular image appear."

"Make that book as real as you possibly can," Maoli instructed. "Don't just produce its appearance but include the kind of energy you want it to contain. Think about how you would like it to affect people."

I brought up all the love I could find and concentrated on how much I wanted to share the information and experiences Daniel had given me. I thought about all the people a book could help. Tears began to run down my face as I remembered the souls I had seen and the limitless encouragement, love, and support they offered to each person on the Earth. I wanted to help everyone who was caught in the clutches of the social mind. I wanted to honor Daniel by making sure that everyone could have the chance to learn the same things I had been blessed to receive. If we could open our hearts and remember who we really were, the Earth would become a place that reflected spirit. Humanity's destiny would finally unfold in the way that it was meant to.

The book floating out in front of me began to fill with magnificent gold and violet light. It vibrated rapidly and grew larger and larger. Then, a wondrous sound came from it, sending a glorious melody out over the circle. "It's so beautiful!" I cried. "It's full of the same kind of energy I saw in my soul."

Maoli was smiling with joy. "If you sustain that form and continue to fill it with the right kind of energy, the idea will come into reality. The energy you put into the form will attract energy that is complimentary to it. Consequently, it will continue to grow larger. Soon, many people will connect their cords to the form. They will communicate what steps must be taken to bring your desire into being. If you pay attention, you will intuitively receive their messages and know how to act in the book's best interests.

"You have to do the work of setting your experiences on paper. You have to act on the information which you receive. If you take the right steps, many people will start to appear in your life with a desire to help with the book. They may not even realize on a conscious level why they want to help. But something deep in their hearts will tell them it's the right thing to do."

"This certainly sheds a new light on goal setting," I said laughing.

"Goals are usually born of the mind and not the heart," Maoli remarked. "That which does not come from your heart is not in accordance with the wishes of your soul. Everything you try to do will fall apart or be unnecessarily difficult."

With a note of irritation, Jessie added, "Remember, even if your social mind tells your nature spirit to create something, it usually adds a negative and contradictory message."

I shook my head. "So, people end up putting negative energy into their form. When they do that, it only attracts the same kind of energy, and it destroys their dreams."

Suddenly, I had the sort of creepy feeling you get when you're being watched. Maoli looked past me with dismay. All the others in the circle looked uneasy. Knowing I had to face whatever it was, I gathered my courage and slowly turned around.

*Jessie began to sing a melody that seemed
ancient and intensely familiar. The glorious
sound didn't come from her mouth, but from deep
within her heart. One by one, the others added
their voices. Some were deep and some soared
like the notes from an opera. Soon, the choir was
perfectly balanced, and the melody was filled
with indescribable love.*

Twenty Five

"Hello, Karen." The woman's voice was haughty and loud.

"You!" I cried, scarcely able to believe she had the guts to come to this place.

"That thing you think you've created is ridiculous," she rasped. "It doesn't exist. I don't see it. No normal person would see it. It's just an unfortunate product of your undisciplined mind."

I pulled up my confidence and tried to sound as powerful as I could. "How did you find me?"

"That's a stupid question," she shot back. "I am you. I go wherever you go."

My social mind marched into the circle and stood in front of me, her back to the fire. Its sparks seemed to shoot outward from her head, producing a frightening appearance that was almost mythical. "These women aren't here to help you," she sneered. "They're propagating a bunch of superstitious nonsense. Mankind is moving forward. Why should we descend into the realm of silly notions about phantoms and spiritual energy?"

Her ugly intrusion produced a surge of adrenaline that roared through my body. I was inches away from rising to my feet and punching her lights out. Then, I heard an almost imperceptible voice. "Remember, Karen. Remember who you really are."

Mistaking my lack of immediate action as an inability to stand up for myself, my social mind launched another attack. "You're being foolish! What makes you think you could even write a book? Why would you waste your time trying? I demand that you get back to reality right this minute! "

From the far side of the circle, I heard the voice again. "Remember who you really are."

I closed my eyes and took a few long, deep breaths. I was in an agonizing battle within myself. The adrenaline screamed through my system, demanding that I act to defend myself. But I knew that resolution of this ugly situation could only come by going into my heart. I continued to try to slow my breathing and let go of the ugly thoughts that urged me to fight.

Then, my social mind began a new, more dangerous campaign. "What about your husband? Don't you suppose he's terribly worried by now? Did you feed the dogs before you left? Are you sure you didn't leave the car lights on? You're awfully hungry by now, aren't you? I know you're thirsty. Isn't it uncomfortable to sit on the ground like that? You're back is hurting; I know it is. What about repaving the driveway? Somebody could fall on that big crack in the middle. Did you renew your insurance?"

I tried desperately to remain focused, but the more my social mind rambled, the harder it became. Before I knew it, she had successfully distracted me from my quest to reach my heart. I started to wonder about each of the things she had brought up. Soon, her questions had multiplied into a thousand ancillary concerns. I opened my eyes and stared into her face. She stopped talking and smiled triumphantly.

"Help me," I whispered, looking beseechingly into the faces of the women in the circle.

Jessie began to sing a melody that seemed ancient and intensely familiar. The glorious sound didn't come from her mouth, but from deep within her heart. One by one, the others added their voices. Some were deep and some soared like the notes from an opera. Soon, the choir was perfectly balanced, and the melody was filled with indescribable love. Without effort, my own heart opened and began to sing. Waves of love gently pushed the adrenaline out through the soles of my feet. My heart swelled with intense joy, and grew beyond the confines of my chest, until it surrounded me in a dazzling cloud of brilliant rose and silver light.

A waterfall of that same light poured over me, heightening my joy, and increasing my strength. As it did, every concern that lingered in my consciousness dissolved into a profound certainty that love was the only thing in the universe that really mattered. And I knew without question that love powered all things, even as it made it possible for me to exist.

My social mind stared at me, her eyes wide with shock. Then she shrugged and seemed to resign herself to her fate. After one last look, she walked out of the circle and disappeared into the night.

*Looking me square in the eye, she said,
"A life that's too full to have time for spirit is
a life that's wasted. I understand that your
modern life has many demands and many
pressures. But remember that Earth's people
spent thousands of years under incredibly
difficult conditions."*

Twenty Six

S till singing, the women didn't look at all surprised that my social mind had left. Now, the woman who had started the song stood up and came toward me. Her dark skin shimmered with the light of the fire. Her deep brown eyes seemed to hold the wisdom of the heavens. Extending her arms up toward the stars, she smiled and offered her thanks to the one who had made her. Then, she turned to me and said, "My name is Enesi. I am from the Xhosa people. Our lands are now contained within the country called South Africa."

"Thank you," I whispered. "Thank you for rescuing me from my social mind."

"You are welcome," she graciously replied. "But it's important that you learn how to go into your natural mind whenever you want to."

"Please," I said urgently. "I want to learn how to do that."

"Let's start with what just happened," she said comfortably. "All things emit a particular frequency of energy. Remember, energy attracts energy that's like itself. When you hear the song of another person's natural mind, you respond by going into your own natural mind. You remember that place within yourself, and move into it, leaving the social mind behind. If you spend your time with those who are caught by their social minds, yours grows stronger."

"But there seem to be so few people on the Earth who live in their natural minds!" I cried.

"There are more people than you know," Enesi answered. "Even people who spend most of their time in the social mind have experiences with their natural mind."

"They do?"

"Certainly," she nodded reassuringly. "Remember, the natural mind isn't something that you have to create. It exists all the time. When a person experiences the kind of love that asks for nothing but wishes only the absolute best for another—whether it be for a lover, a friend, a child, or an animal—she is experiencing the natural mind."

"Many people have this experience when they go into nature. Away from machines and the demands of ordinary life, they find themselves responding to the beauty around them in a way that's very different. "

She paused, then pointed toward the glittering canopy above us. "Haven't you ever sat beneath the night sky and become absorbed in the stars? If you don't insist on naming the constellations or become engaged in considering scientific theories about how the universe came to exist, your mind will slow. When you allow yourself to take the time to sit quietly, and witness the awesome beauty moving above you, something inside you begins to awaken. You start to realize that whatever your personal concerns, the cosmos continues to proceed as it should. It's all under the direction of a divine force—the same force that cares for you."

"I've had that feeling when I've been by the ocean," I replied. "It's a special realization that the things that are aggravating, the people I have conflicts with, the worries I have, are all pretty small compared to the power contained in the sea. Sometimes, I've gotten so relaxed, it almost feels like I'm a part of the ocean."

"And you've had some different kinds of experiences on the beach, as well," Enesi stated.

I shifted uncomfortably. "I have to admit, there have been times where I've looked forward to a peaceful, solitary walk, only to find that I am hardly present once I get there. I've walked miles and practically ignored my surroundings. All I accomplished was outdoor agitation. I've only been aware of the bee's nest of worries buzzing in my head."

"Those are perfect examples of what it's like to be in your natural mind, and what happens when you enter your social mind. The power of the sea, the fragrance of salt water, the seagulls laughing overhead—all that never moved. It's you who change when you shift your consciousness from the false mind into the natural mind."

"My social mind is so powerful! You saw what happened to me. I couldn't help myself."

"Your social mind has been allowed to do exactly as she wishes for many, many years. Consequently, she has gained power and exerts control over you. The minute she begins to talk, you automatically listen. But you have given her the power she has. She doesn't have ultimate control. You do."

"How do I take back my power? What can I do?"

"There are thousands of ways to practice entering your natural mind," she answered. "But they all require two essential things."

"What are they?"

"Time and commitment," Enesi replied.

"Difficult commodities in my culture," I responded glumly.

Looking me square in the eye, she said, "A life that's too full to have time for spirit is a life that's wasted. I understand that your modern life has many demands and many pressures. But remember that Earth's people spent thousands of years under incredibly difficult conditions." Her voice full of compassion, she continued. "It wasn't easy to survive when the rains didn't come, and the land dried up. There was plenty of pressure when there were children to care for, and the men were gone for weeks at a time. When the water had to be carried from the river, and shelter had to be scratched out of the ground, they were busy beyond description."

Ashamed, I nodded my head and waited for her to tell me more. "Yet, they always made time to honor spirit. They were committed to maintaining the link between spirit and themselves. They understood that without spirit, they were nothing."

"I guess most of us choose to dedicate our lives to the social mind," I stated sadly. "If I make the time and nurture the commitment, then what do I do?"

"Oh, for heaven's sake," a strong voice came from my right. "Let me get her started."

Twenty Seven

Abundantly streaked with gray, the woman's bright yellow hair swirled around her face. She was very tall and large-boned. Her arms were prolifically freckled and looked as though they had spent many years doing physical labor. "Hi," she said with a hearty smile. "I'm Sally. It's time to get down to business."

After talking to the women from unfamiliar cultures, I was surprised to find an ordinary American in the gathering. But, despite her appearance and way of speaking, she radiated a special energy that made her beautiful. I knew her heart was full of love.

"I'm just a big, 'ol farm gal from Minnesota. But I can help you out. I learned a long time ago how to find my right mind. A real nice fella came through my little town. Everybody thought he was strange, but I found him fascinating. Anyway, what he told me made a lot of sense and I've been practicing it ever since."

"I'm ready," I replied.

"I'm going to give you some real simple steps to take. Like Enesi said, you have to make the time and the commitment to work at it. But I promise you won't be disappointed. My word, when I think about what my life was like before I could hear my soul, it just makes me shudder."

"How long have you been able to hear your soul, Sally?" I asked.

"Well," she grinned. "You have to understand it took me some time to really get free of that darned social mind. Golly, it came after me with a vengeance. But I knew I had to keep going toward what I wanted, no matter how many things got in the way."

"What do I do?"

"Out here, there's plenty of peace and quiet. When you start practicing at home, you're going to have to find yourself a private place. Shoot, a closet will work just fine. Or you can go in the bathroom and lock the door. Of course, if you can go into the great outdoors, you'll be surrounded by good energy, so that's the best thing. But I know that's not always possible. Just find a place where you won't be bothered by anybody."

"Okay," I said. My life was incredibly busy, but I could certainly find some time to be alone.

"Lay yourself down," she said, pushing me very gently on my shoulders. "Now, put your arms out to the sides. Close your eyes and breathe."

I did as I was told, but after a few minutes Sally said, "That's not breathing, girl." She put one large hand on the lower part of my abdomen and said, "Make sure you breathe way down here. Lift my hand up with your belly."

I took in a big breath and allowed the air to push my belly against her hand. It was an unfamiliar feeling. I realized I had spent years trying to hold my stomach in as much as I could. It had resulted in an unnatural way of breathing up high in my chest and throat.

"That's real good," Sally said encouragingly. "Now, I want you to just bring your attention to your breaths as they enter and leave your body. Just do that for a few minutes. I'll be quiet."

The more air I took in, the more my body relaxed. Soon, my breaths were long and slow. Still, my mind sent up a steady chatter of half-formed concerns. I wondered what Sally would say next. I worried that I wasn't breathing correctly. I thought about whether people were looking for me in Boise.

Sally spoke again, but her voice was now low and gentle. "Karen, begin to cast your thoughts away. Don't argue with them. Just invite them to leave this very special time. It's helpful to talk to your thoughts as though they are people who want your attention. Acknowledge them and tell them you will listen to what they have to say when you have finished."

Not following her instruction, I tried to tell myself that all my thoughts were gone. They scurried around my mind like an unruly pack of squirrels. Disappointed, I lost the rhythm of my breathing and tensed.

"Remember," Sally whispered. "Don't fight with yourself. Don't tell yourself something that isn't true. Just invite your thoughts to go and wait somewhere else."

This time, I did as I was told. Surprisingly, my thoughts slowed and there were spaces of time between them. I continued to focus on the rhythm of my breathing and gently ushered each new thought off into the distance.

After several minutes, Sally said, "Now, begin to pay attention to the small space between your breaths. Notice that it's very quiet and still in the place between your exhalation and the inhalation of a new breath." She let me take twenty more breaths and added, "As your rhythm slows, this space will grow longer and longer. Pull your attention more and more into this peaceful place."

I was beginning to drift on waves of relaxation. The boundaries of my body had melted, and it was no longer clear where I ended, and the ground began. Occasional thoughts still intruded, but I was able to gently send them away. I had started to look forward to the experience of being between the breaths. When I was forced to take in air, I was almost disappointed to have to leave this special place. A wonderful sense of peacefulness spread over me like a soft blanket.

"As you explore the space between the breaths, begin to notice that it's filled with a special energy. The energy pours into the space from a source that seems to be outside of you. Just feel this energy and offer gratitude for its presence. Don't try to do anything with it. Simply watch it flow into the space."

Now, my breaths were far apart. I was able to spend quite a long time in the space between them. I could feel the energy that Sally had mentioned. It was very different than that of my usual life. It seemed to be filled with love and vibrated quickly and joyfully. Each time I came back to the space, I gratefully drank in more of the beautiful energy that existed there. My heart seemed to receive it, and relaxed and opened itself, like a flower in the sunshine.

Sally did not speak for many minutes. Then she whispered, "Don't change the rhythm of your breathing. Very gently, and very slowly, open your eyes."

I stared up at the stars with a profound sense of tranquility and gratitude. Filled with love, my heart seemed too big for my chest. Slowly, I sat up and looked around the circle. Each woman smiled at me, and their beauty had increased. Their hearts glowed underneath their clothing, sending out a soft yellow light. I was reminded again that everything that exists has at its core a powerful form of love.

I was directed to lay back and close my eyes and continue as I had before. Sally said, "Remember, your heart constantly receives beautiful, sustaining energy from your highest self. Offer your gratitude. Enjoy the gift you are given. Draw that love into every corner of your being."

Basking in the warmth and joy of the energy, I silently praised my soul. Tears rolled down my face, as I realized again that it extended its love to me through all the days of my life. It was me who turned away and hid inside the realm of my social mind.

Sally directed me through the process many times. I became more and more able to find that space by myself. Each time I sat up, she said the same thing, "As your eyes open, focus on keeping your consciousness within the beautiful space between the breaths. Bring that sense of tranquility and spaciousness with you as you move back out into your world. Remember that each person is also a container for those energies of love and beauty. Watch for the movement of that energy within them."

I was amazed that the natural mind was so easy for me to find. "Sally, this isn't complicated at all! I can't believe that none of us are taught how to do it right from the beginning of our lives."

"Remember," she said soberly, "you're here with us. Each person in this circle is helping you by sending out the energy of her natural mind. I'm afraid it's a lot harder when you spend most of your time around a lot of social minds. And," she added emphatically, "it all depends on you making the time and the commitment to practice."

"The key is to gain enough familiarity with the natural mind. That way, you can go into it and leave the social mind behind, no matter what she comes up with to fight you."

"Is there ever any reason to argue with her?" I asked, trying to find another way to bring understanding to this obnoxious part of myself.

"No," Sally answered strongly. "There's only one way to get rid of the social mind, and that's by finding your natural mind."

Now filled with the energy from my soul, I was confident. But what she said next caught me completely by surprise.

Every time I had to return to the realm of my social mind, it felt as though I was suffocating. The energy there was thick and slow moving. It made me fearful and drained my strength. My natural mind was so spacious and clean, so filled with love and hope, it was hard to imagine that I could ever willingly want to leave it.

Twenty Eight

"Okay, darlin', it's time to invite that social mind right back here."

"What?" I said, my jaw tensing. "I don't want her to be anywhere near me!"

"Got to practice," Sally replied. "You know and I know, as soon as you go back to the regular world, she's gonna show up. You might as well learn how to deal with her."

Seeing that Sally wasn't about to back down, I nodded my head in agreement. "How do I bring her back?"

She roared with laughter. "You already know how to do that! Just start thinking about something you don't like about yourself. Or think about another person you're mad at. That'll bring her back here for sure."

I did as I was told, amazed to find how difficult it was to find those feelings again. They were so contrary to the energy in my heart. Formerly habitual, the emotions of anger, condemnation and judgment seemed totally foreign. I felt like I was pouring oil into a pure mountain stream.

Sure enough, it wasn't long before I heard that irritating voice of my social mind. "Well, I see you've come to your senses," she sneered. "I knew you'd want me back. Without me, you can't live."

Raging at her presumptive, judging, angry attitude, I climbed to my feet and prepared to defend myself. I was about to launch a speech about how much I had learned about how to find my natural mind, when I stopped myself. Instead, I lay back down on the ground and closed my eyes. This time, I had an already practiced path by which to escape. Now, I knew where I needed to go, and what I would find there when I achieved my goal. I pulled up a ferocious desire to reach my natural mind and focused on my practice.

Suddenly, my social mind's voice was gone. It was replaced by a sense of enormous peace and absolute quiet. Once again, I felt powerful love rain over me and fill me with sparkling energy. My heart relaxed and opened, knowing it had nothing to fear.

"That's real good. Now, do it again."

Sally directed me to practice shifting back and forth between my social mind and my natural mind a hundred times or more. When she finally stopped, I had increased my ability to find my natural mind under duress. I had become very familiar with the differences between the two types of energy that each mind possessed.

Every time I had to return to the realm of my social mind, it felt as though I was suffocating. The energy there was thick and slow moving. It made me fearful and drained my strength. My natural mind was so spacious and clean, so filled with love and hope, it was hard to imagine that I could ever willingly want to leave it. But I still had a lot of questions. "Sally, I know how beautiful my natural mind is, but it doesn't seem to be very concerned with the demands of ordinary life. As much as I'd like to, I can't sit around all day just enjoying my blissful experiences."

To my chagrin, Sally laughed uproariously. "Oh boy! That's a good one."

My feelings were hurt. "What's so funny?"

"Can't you see?" she challenged. "That question's coming straight from your social mind. It's the best argument it has. It tells you that it's your source of strength. But it gives you the feelings that you then think you need the social mind to conquer. Giving up the social mind doesn't lead to a loss of self, but an increased sense of your true self. Feeling weak, insecure, undervalued, or unappreciated all stem from a reliance on the social mind."

"I'm not sure I understand."

"What you call a strong, healthy ego is the result of fulfilling the list of requirements your social mind dictates to you. When you don't perform, it turns on you, blames you, and depreciates you. Then, you suffer from low self-esteem, and you try even harder to do what it tells you is essential."

"But I have things I want to do! I don't think they all come from my social mind."

Maoli spoke up. "Let me see if I can help with an example. It's common in your culture for people to base their self-esteem on earning a good living. When they do, they feel very good about themselves. But what happens if through no fault of their own, they lose their jobs? All that self-esteem vanishes in an instant. It was based on what the social mind told them was their proof of value."

"So, you're saying that the social mind sets us up for disaster by making sure our self-esteem is based on fulfilling things that are dependent on the world outside of ourselves."

"Exactly. Your sense of self-value should be based on the knowledge that you are a constantly cherished child of the soul. Whatever you may choose to do with your time on Earth, your soul never changes in its love for you. You are worthy of its love simply because you exist. You don't have to earn its feelings about you, and nothing you can do will alter those feelings."

"So, if we draw our strength and sense of being a good person from the soul, it sounds like nothing that happens in our life can shake us. We can meet all our challenges with the certainty that we are fed by an everlasting love, and a bountiful source of strength and wisdom."

"Right. When you already have strength, and you know in your deepest heart that you are a beautiful creation of the divine, you can make your decisions about how to spend your time on the Earth freely. You aren't constantly trying to prove your worth. You can relax in the awareness that you already have what you truly need."

"This reminds me of a friend I had in grade school." I said sadly. "She had a very critical father. Her dad only gave her love when she did well in school. As long as she got 'A's', her father praised her and even spent time with her. But one semester she got the chickenpox and missed a few weeks of school. Her grades dropped, and her father punished her mercilessly. Pretty soon, she was so terrified of failure she froze up and couldn't learn much of anything."

"The social mind at work," Sally said disgustedly. "That child became weak, even though her father thought he was developing strength in her. Wouldn't it have been better if he had showered love over her, and reminded her about what a capable girl she was?"

"Without a doubt," I replied. "It sounds like the social mind keeps us on a miserable cycle of triumph and failure, while the natural mind keeps us feeling strong and steady. With the love of our soul as a base, we can accomplish far more than we can if we're spending a lot of time licking our wounds and feeling bad about ourselves."

When I was really honest with myself, ordinary life could be pretty scary when I insisted on remaining in the social mind. I was always anxious about something. If life was going well and I couldn't find anything to worry about, then I'd get scared about growing old and dying someday.

Jessie piped up. "Look at somebody like Mother Theresa! She was in her natural mind almost all the time. She didn't sit in a corner and bliss out. She used the love from her soul to fuel her work in the world. She met obstacles with ultimate strength."

Enesi offered, "The natural mind can see the rules and expectations of your culture and infuse them with light and love. Someone like Mother Teresa, or the Dalai Lama doesn't charge into the environment and ignore the cultural environment. They have the freedom to work in a fluid way within the context of any society."

"But I'm not Mother Teresa! Those are awfully big shoes to fill!"

"Oh, Karen," Jessie replied. "Haven't you ever known someone who goes through life with a sense of peacefulness and ease? No matter what befalls him, he maintains his serenity and balance. It doesn't matter what kind of work he's doing, or what he wants to achieve, he does everything with unwavering strength and absolute love."

I thought for a moment. I did know a few people like that. They were amazing. And they managed to accomplish wonderful things in the world. I laughed. "Daniel told me that all things change when I change. It sounds like all things change when I shift from my social mind into my natural mind."

Sally proclaimed, "It's the social mind and its need to concretize life that makes for the epidemic of anxiety and depression in our country! People are constantly afraid that they won't measure up, and even if they do, they're left with a terrible emptiness inside. If you do exactly what your social mind demands, it takes up all the room you have. Your soul can't find a way in. The result is a sense of meaninglessness. People who don't have it always think that money will solve their pain. People who have money know that it doesn't fix the pain in their hearts."

I thought for a moment. "Money isn't contrary to spirit, is it?"

Sally howled. "Money is money. There's nothing wrong with having it, but if the pursuit of money is your purpose for living, you're going to be one sad duck."

Jessie said gently, "Your purpose on the Earth is to infuse everything you do with the light and love of spirit. You can bring sacredness to all of your interactions, and all of your tasks. When my people plant corn, it is a sacred event, because we make it so.

You can throw the kernels into the ground and go about your business. Or you can acknowledge the power and beauty of life and tenderly tuck every new plant under its blanket of earth. Maybe the resulting crop will be the same, no matter which you do...but you won't be the same."

"Thank you," I offered gratefully. "You've really helped me to understand."

"All right, ladies," Sally announced. "She's ready for the next step!"

Twenty Nine

Enesi produced a tall drum, beautifully decorated with bright beads, and the feathers from many kinds of birds. When she began to pound, it had a deeply resonate sound. Soon, Jessie had joined her with a smaller drum, painted with red, blue, and yellow symbols. Together, they created an intricate, compelling rhythm that inspired my body to move.

Pulling me to my feet, Maoli began to dance. Her wide feet forcefully hitting the ground, she went clockwise around the circle. At the three o'clock position, she stopped and raised her arms high above her head. Then, a low note came from deep within her and gradually increased until it became the loudest sound she could make. She did the same thing at the six and nine o'clock positions of the circle. When she arrived back at the top, she called out her praise to the one who had made her and continued moving again.

She beckoned me to join her, and I did as she did. When I made the sounds, it seemed that a different kind of energy was being heightened at each point. I knew without asking, that this was a ceremony which honored the three spirits that made my being, and the soul from which we had come.

Jessie and Enesi drummed faster and faster. All of our hearts transcended their soft glow and became brilliant, white beacons that illuminated the area all around us. Suddenly, I could see the energy of the three spirits around each of the women. The nature spirits' seemed to be in a state of ecstasy. Their energy sparkled and danced in a whirlwind of joy. The natural minds' were filled with pure, clear platinum and golden light.

My feet skipped across the ground in an amazing tribute to

the rhythm of the drums, until it seemed I couldn't possibly hold any more happiness without exploding. Then, the boundaries of my being seemed to disappear, until it felt as though we were all one powerful woman. The fire in our midst was our soul. I could feel the abilities of all of us and knew all the joys and sorrows that life had brought us.

Finally, dawn beckoned over the horizon, and we sat close to one another. Putting our hands together, each woman offered one more gift to me. Maoli spoke first. "My people are reminded of their natural mind by staring into a waterfall, gazing into an empty sky, or dancing."

Jessie smiled and said, "My people use the drum, the dance, looking into the fire, or going alone to the sacred places.

The tiny bush woman said, "My people remember always. We know no other kind of mind."

Enesi grasped my hand tightly. "We practice by moving the location of 'me' from our head to different parts of our bodies. Sometimes, it is the thumb who becomes 'me' and regards the head as an appendage. In this way, we remember that our being does not live within our brain but is something much bigger than that."

The Tibetan smiled in appreciation and said, "We use our singing bowls to remind us. They are made of metal, and when struck, send out a glorious sound. We also repeat the same sound with our voices over and over, until we are brought back to the center of our being."

"We practice by identifying with nature," the Celtic woman said. "All around us, trees, flowers, birds, and animals remind us of our being. Often, we start by imagining that we are a flower, a rock, or the river. We concentrate on what it is like to be that natural thing. What is it like to have fragrant petals, or a smooth, hard surface, or rush endlessly toward the sea? After a while our 'self' has been abandoned, and we see our body as the thing being watched."

Mariah offered, "We often practice in complete darkness. We keep our eyes open, and images from our minds project themselves to fill up the emptiness. One by one, we send the projections away, until our mind becomes perfectly still."

A hearty chuckle told me Sally was about to say something. "I don't do anything fancy. Sometimes, I just keep my concentration right on what I'm doing. I don't allow it to go all over the place. It helps to do something real repetitive—I have lots of things to choose from on the farm. Mostly, I do exactly what I taught you to do. Takes me about fifteen or twenty minutes. Like I said, you have to keep at it, but it works."

Tears spilled over my face, and I thanked each one of them for helping me to learn. I would never forget their strength, love, and knowledge. Jessie told me to stay where I was, and the others got up and went into her home. She pulled me to my feet and gave me a tight hug. "You can do it, Karen. I know you can." I watched her go around the big trunk of the oak tree, but she never emerged out the other side. Taking a few steps toward it, I was stopped by the sound of a familiar voice.

"Hi, Karen." I whirled around to find Daniel's adult form, a sparkling smile on his face.

"Daniel!" I cried. "Where have you been? I've learned so much from my wonderful new friends. Jessie is right over there...at least I think she is. Come over to the house and meet them."

He didn't answer but looked toward Jessie's home. I had turned around, expecting to see the women gathered on the porch. Now, too stunned to speak, I began to tremble. Daniel's comforting hand came to my shoulder, and he said, "You have done very well, Karen. Very well, indeed."

Daniel had led me through three heavens in our first meetings. Filled with awesome beauty and astounding love, they each had a special purpose.

♥

Thirty

"What happened?" The walls of Jessie's home leaned inward and barely supported the collapsed roof. The white paint was gone; the boards were sun-bleached and worn. Her garden lay in tangled confusion, and the absent front door allowed dust to blow through the house.

With an overwhelming sense of grief, I turned back to Daniel. "Where are they? What happened to the house?" It was only a second before better questions popped in my mind. "Who were those women, Daniel? Or maybe I should ask, what were they?"

"Jessie was what many people would call an angel," Daniel replied, watching me carefully.

I was flabbergasted. "An angel? I thought you said that angels didn't exist!"

"Oh, angels do exist," he said with a smile.

"What about the rest of the women? Were they all angels, too?"

"No, Karen," he replied. "All the others currently have bodies on the Earth. But they didn't bring them to Jessie's house."

"What?" I had no idea what he was trying to tell me.

"By working hard to destroy their social minds, and by learning to be in constant connection to their souls, they were able to project their images to this place."

Somewhere along the way, my mouth had dropped open. "Are you saying they were sitting in different parts of the world, and communicating with me at the same time?"

Daniel grinned. "In the world of spirit, time and space don't exist. You're amazed only because most of humankind has not yet recovered their natural, spiritual abilities. Remember, talking to someone on the other side of the Earth seemed impossible before the telephone became commonplace."

"Wow." Letting myself sink onto the ground, I knew I was nowhere near being able to learn how to do that. I went on to a safer topic. "Tell me about angels, Daniel."

"There are many different levels of angels. Many have never had a physical body. Some, like Jessie, have had many, many lifetimes on the Earth. She lived her last lifetime in that house until 1964."

"Tell me more," I urged.

"What you call an angel is a direct projection of the soul."

My heart began its familiar pounding in the presence of Daniel. "I don't understand."

He continued, "Rather than sending three spirits to inhabit a physical body, the soul simply sends a representation of itself onto the Earth."

"Why would a soul do such a thing?"

He smiled, "Do you remember seeing the different realms in heaven?"

"Of course I do! How could I ever forget?" Daniel had led me through three heavens in our first meetings. Filled with awesome beauty and astounding love, they each had a special purpose. The first heaven contained the souls of most of humanity. Those souls congregated in communities of purpose and sent lifetimes to the Earth. In the second heaven, the souls were at a higher level of spiritual development. Although they still had individual identities, they worked together as one, loving community. They helped the members of the first heaven in their process of growth. In the third heaven, the souls were no longer separated but had dissolved into one limitless heart. They fed the first two heavens with a continuous shower of energy and love. Daniel had taken me to the edge of still another heaven, but we had stopped there. I knew there was something of unimaginable proportions waiting there, but I didn't know what it was.

"The souls who live in the second heaven continue to grow. Eventually, they are ready to enter the third heaven and no longer need to send lifetimes to the Earth. But they have great love and continual concern for Earth's people. Sometimes, they choose to help someone by temporarily appearing to them for a specific purpose. Then, the projection is withdrawn."

"That's amazing!" I exclaimed. "Jessie seemed as real as I am."

"Remember," Daniel said somberly. "There are many things affecting the Earth. They're not always what they appear to be. It's very dangerous to be naive."

I stared at him for a moment, and then asked, "What kinds of things?"

Out of nowhere, a swirling cloud of dust appeared. I buried my head between my knees and closed my eyes. When I opened them, my surroundings were completely different.

Denial is an interesting thing. I had spent years as a counselor trying to break through that peculiar ability human beings have when they are uncomfortable with the reality staring them in the face.

♥

Thirty One

Violet and soft yellow light moved around me in a circular motion. It seemed that Daniel was no longer with me. But it wasn't long before I heard an unfamiliar voice.

"Do you know where we are?"

Peering into the light, I tried to find the owner of the question. Deciding to take a few steps forward, I could just see a human shape moving toward me. "Hello?" I called, not sure I wanted to find out who was there.

"Do you know where we are?" Now, the vague outline had assumed the appearance of a woman. Hastening to meet me, she seemed worried.

"Who are you?" I cautiously questioned. This was certainly not the first time I had encountered the unexpected. Involuntarily, I braced myself for whatever this stranger brought with her.

"I'm Elizabeth Hansen. Who are you?" She said, sounding like an uncomfortable introvert at a dinner party.

"I'm Karen," I replied, then stopped. What was the appropriate thing to say under these circumstances?

"It's been so long since I've seen anybody..." she trailed off. Then, taking a deep breath she said, "I'm a little confused right now. This is awfully embarrassing, but I don't seem to know where I am."

Now close enough to see, Elizabeth was an ordinary woman. Probably in her late sixties, she was dressed in a navy blue pantsuit. Her white earrings and carefully arranged silvery hair created the impression she was on her way to have lunch with her friends. Her anxious brown eyes sought an answer I didn't have. What the devil was she doing here?

This is some kind of Daniel trick, I thought, careful not to let my guard down. Glancing away from her for a moment, I looked behind me and tried to find him. Surprisingly, the air in that direction had changed. Now much lighter, I could see quite far into the distance. But Daniel was nowhere to be seen.

"Do you know where we are?" Elizabeth asked plaintively, trying to regain my attention.

"Well, I thought I did," I answered. "But I think we're somewhere different now." Although what I had said was true, it also served as a good evasion. If she didn't know we weren't in Kansas anymore, I sure didn't want to be the one to have explain it to her.

"Daniel," I moaned silently. "Please don't stick me with this one. I don't know what to do with her!" Then it occurred to me, maybe Elizabeth was another of Daniel's students. Tentatively, I asked, "Do you know Daniel?"

"Daniel Levinson, of course I do," she replied brightly. "He's a lovely man. Where did you meet him?"

"No...not Daniel Levinson," I said carefully. "You know, *Daniel*. Did he bring you here?"

"I don't think so," she said. "The only Daniel I know is Daniel Levinson." Then looking painfully puzzled, she added, "But, this is the strangest thing, the last thing I can recall is getting in my car to meet my daughter for tea."

Who knows what Daniel is up to, I thought. Then, compassion swept through me, and I held out my hand for her to take. "Let's go this way," I offered. Gratefully, she placed a small, carefully manicured hand into mine. I had no idea where we were going, but the way ahead seemed much brighter and more clear.

As we walked toward the easier air, I felt more comfortable. "Where are you from?" I inquired politely.

"Oh, I'm originally from Wyoming, but I've spent the last

twenty years in California," she replied. "My husband worked in the defense industry. He died three years ago."

Sparkling particles of lilac began to swirl around us, delicately landing on my arms. Ahead, the environment revealed itself like a meadow emerging from the fog in late morning. So much brighter, it beckoned with the promise of incredible beauty. I picked up our pace, glad to be going in the right direction. Elizabeth seemed content to continue by my side.

This is the worst exercise in denial I've ever been a part of, I thought to myself. We're in the middle of some kind of energy, nothing normal to be seen anywhere, and we're acting like two people walking across a simple suburban park.

Denial is an interesting thing. I had spent years as a counselor trying to break through that peculiar ability human beings have when they are uncomfortable with the reality staring them in the face. I thought often about a Monty Python movie I had seen. A knight in battle has his limbs successively removed by his opponent. Every time a terrible injury is inflicted, the attacker points out his awful accomplishment and the victim replies, "No you haven't!" This goes on until the poor fellow is reduced to hopping around on his trunk. Still, he insists nothing has happened. That's denial. It's our way of surviving by keeping some version of reality that we can live with intact in our mind, no matter what the contrary evidence might be.

Elizabeth broke in, "Where are you from?"

"I'm from Boise," I said quietly, not quite willing to confront the obvious issue.

"Oh, Boise is a nice city," she replied. "I used to visit there often."

Deciding to make a small attempt to break through to the reality at hand, I asked, "How did you get here?"

Confusion registered in her face as she said, "You know, I don't remember. I don't remember at all."

I certainly had no idea how she had gotten to this place. I wasn't completely sure where we were, either. But, glad to have some company, I looked around with relief at our surroundings. A beautiful expanse lay before us. Glittering particles of rose and aqua light blew across gently rolling hills like snowdrifts in an easy breeze.

Taking a deep breath of clear air, I began to smile. This place seemed so happy. The atmosphere was filled with a certain sweetness, like the smile of a little girl enjoying a sunny day.

"My, I do feel better," Elizabeth said cheerfully. "Let's just stop and stay here a while." With that, she carefully arranged herself on a gentle little slope.

Now convinced my companion wasn't about to leap out of disguise and throw me over an emotional precipice, I sat with her and relaxed.

That was a mistake.

Thirty Two

"I live here! Get out!" The shout came from behind a small hill to our left.

Shocked to find anyone else in this beautiful place, Elizabeth and I scrambled to our feet.

There he was. At least eighty years old, he walked with a jagged limp. Eyes narrowed in irritation; he waved his arms like someone trying to shoo away an unwanted dog.

"Get the hell out of here! This place is mine!"

"Wait a minute!" I yelled, trying to stop his advance. Elizabeth had taken shelter behind my back. "Come on, let's talk."

"Talk! I don't want to talk to you. You're in my place, now get out!" Now only a few yards away, his pale gray eyes were livid. What in the world was he so upset about? Surely, this place couldn't really belong to him.

I put out my hand in gesture of conciliation. Ignoring it, he continued his tirade, "Damn it, I've got a place and I'm not giving it up to the two of you!"

"Sir," I said calmly, feeling Elizabeth shaking against my back. "We don't want to take anything from you. We don't even know where we are!"

Like hell you don't," he replied. "I've seen the likes of you before. Next thing you know, there's not enough for me." Wobbling on well-used legs, he began to wheeze. "You see? Already I don't have enough to get by."

"Enough?" I replied without a clue about what he was referring to.

"Enough energy, damn it!" he shouted.

Looking around, I could see there had been a curious change

in our environment. The brightness had dimmed a little and the atmosphere seemed less comfortable somehow. Directly around the stranger, the air seemed thick and muddled.

"Look," I said in a futile attempt to calm him down. "I don't really understand what's happening here. We don't know where we are or how we got here. If you'll just be patient for a minute, we'll be on our way."

"You don't know how you got here," he repeated, sarcasm thick in his voice. He looked disgusted and said, "Another pair of lost idiots!"

I replied defensively, "Yes, I did say we were lost. And that we don't know how we got here."

His laughter went a notch higher, and his voice sounded like an angry thirteen-year-old taunting a schoolmate. "You're dead, stupid. That's how you got here. You're just plain dead."

Thirty Three

Aghast at his statement, I stared at him while he chuckled over my obvious discomfort. Behind me, Elizabeth had started to sob. Reaching back, I tried to comfort her as best I could.

Taking great pleasure in Elizabeth's distress, the old man slowly drove his point straight into her heart, "Yep. You're just plain, permanently, awfully, dead."

Angry at his complete lack of compassion, I shouted, "Stop it! Just stop it! I know for a fact that this is not death! Death isn't anything like this!"

"And just how would you know that?" he mockingly replied. Shaggy gray eyebrows arched high; he waited for my answer.

Now what do I say, I thought, unsure about how much this cruel man knew. Could I really start explaining the fact that I had traveled into the heavens? Should I tell him about the incredible love that waited for all people after death? Feeling Elizabeth shaking uncontrollably, I knew I had to try.

Momentarily fumbling for a way to break through to him, I decided to just speak the truth, "Look, I've been to places that you are apparently very confused about. Death isn't anything like this."

My answer only powered his horrible self-confidence, "You think you're awfully smart. Just where in the hell do you think you are?"

I was temporarily stopped. The fact was, I didn't have a clue about where we were.

Seeing a gorgeous, rainbow-hued cloud of light floating by the man opened his mouth wide and sucked it in. Like a thirsty animal after a long walk, he drew long and hard, the energy disappearing down his throat. Suddenly bigger, he grinned maddeningly over at me and said, "I know exactly where I am."

Still stunned by what I had just seen, I said cautiously, "Well, tell me then. Just where are we?"

Pulling himself to full height, he announced, "We're inside Joe Delario, idiot."

Thirty Four

Watching him take in another enormous drink of beautiful energy, I managed to squeak, "Who's Joe Delario?"

"Just some stupid person," he snarled. "But he's got a lot of really good energy."

Struggling to understand, I asked, "How could we possibly be inside him?"

There was that awful laugh again, "By being dead! I keep trying to tell you, you're dead." After waiting for my non-existent response, he continued, "He's alive, but we're all dead. He's got energy, we don't. What he's got, I've got, and I'm not about to share it with you."

"How did you get here?" I asked, deciding to try to learn from this awful creature.

"Died," he said simply. "Next thing I knew, I had to find some way to feed myself and there he was."

"But didn't you see your soul? Didn't you find her?"

"Nope. Didn't see nothing like that, never have, never will. There's energy, and those of us who need it. That's it, end of the story," he replied with an attitude of terrible finality. "Furthermore, I'm not going out there to look for any other living person to feed from. Too much trouble. This one's good."

How could this be? I had seen the awesome beauty of the soul. I had been held in his arms! I had felt his touch. How in the world did this guy end up here?

"Does Joe know you're here?" I asked, not knowing for the moment what else to say.

"Of course not," he answered haughtily.

"So, you aren't here by invitation?" I challenged, remembering that Daniel had once told me the spiritual rule was, 'one body, one soul.'

"Nope, but it don't matter to me. I get what I need. That's all I worry about."

"So, this energy is always available to you?"

"So far. Oh, Joe has his down times, and then things get tough for me. But so far, so good," he replied, clearly feeling pleased about his situation.

"Down times?" I questioned.

"Yeah. There's really only enough energy in his system to keep him going. When I take what I need, he gets a little weak, like somebody who gives too much blood." There was no hint of compassion for how he might be affecting Joe.

"And," he continued, "I've noticed he's starting to take after me a bit. Makes it really good in here. He's starting to do things I used to do when I was alive."

"You can see him?" I asked sharply. "You can watch what he does?"

"Oh sure," he said gleefully. "I get to do everything he does. Some of it's pretty good—like with the wife, you know. She's an awfully pretty gal." He grinned lustily, and I felt Elizabeth shudder.

"Wait a minute, why would he start doing the same things you used to do when you were alive?" I asked, feeling tremendously aggravated by his attitude.

"Well," he said, lowering his voice. "I just keep asking, just keep whispering in his ear, just keep showing up in his dreams, and just keep mixing what's left of me in with his energy. Next thing you know, he's off doing things he never thought to do on his own."

Suddenly, I had an overwhelming feeling of creepy discomfort, like being in someone's house uninvited. I wanted to leave this place, this terrible man and poor Joe. To think that this old man could influence a living person's behavior was appalling!

"Come on, Elizabeth," I said, pulling her from behind me. "We need to get out of here." Still trembling, she clutched my arm and hastily agreed to go. But go where? I had no idea about how to get out of here.

The man knew that and taunted me with the fact, "Where are you going to go? There's only one way out of here, but you'll have to find another live person to attach to."

"You're like some kind of vampire," I said angrily. "What right do you have to suck away someone else's energy? Joe should be the one to decide what he wants to do with his life!"

"What do you expect me to do?" he shot back. For the first time, I saw a momentary flash of self-pity in his eyes.

I didn't have an answer for him. I knew he belonged in the arms of his soul, but I didn't know why he wasn't already there. What had happened to allow him to be like this? Furthermore, I didn't know how to fix it.

It had always been hard for me to see someone in pain without trying to fix it for them. I went through complicated mental gymnastics every time it happened, never satisfied if I couldn't come up with an answer. Over the years, I had practiced staying out of a codependent role with people; after all, what people created in their lives was really their responsibility to sort out, not mine. But it bothered me.

This situation was clearly wrong. I didn't know Joe, but whoever he was, he was certainly entitled to have his own energy and use it in his own way. This ugly man was violating some cosmic rule. I had no doubt about that. But I didn't have any clear answers.

"Help, Daniel," I called silently. "Please, help me. I can't figure it out for myself. I truly can't."

"Look!" Elizabeth suddenly cried out.

My sight following the direction of her pointed finger, I gazed out into the distance.

And there, I found the answers.

*The light from the doorway had increased
and now washed over us in splendid
profusion. The voice began to sing, each
gentle note was so filled with love,
"Come...come my dear one.
Please come home..."*

Thirty Five

Like a window that has suddenly been opened, the entrance into another reality revealed itself before us. Almost twenty feet away, brilliant platinum light shot through the opening in wide, shimmering rays. Inside, I could make out a multitude of figures that swayed gently in a dazzling, incandescent breeze.

Enraptured, Elizabeth had already started to walk slowly toward the threshold, a smile spreading across her face. My own heart swelled in recognition as soft voices began to call, "Come... come my sweet creation."

An intense sensation of the purest kind of love permeated my being. Intoxicated with the glorious feeling, I had just started to follow her when the old man's screams jolted me out of my joyful reverie. "God! Oh my God! There they are again!"

Filled with fear, his words were a startling contrast to the profound energies of love streaming out to greet us. Reluctantly, I turned away from the gateway to look at him.

Trying too hard to flee on legs that couldn't cooperate, he had fallen down. He cowered in terror; pitiful groans came from deep within him.

"What's wrong? They are here! Don't be afraid!" I cried, completely convinced we were being called by our souls.

"No!" he screamed. "No...no...no!" Frantically, he attempted to crawl away. His weakened body quickly collapsed on the ground.

I knelt down beside him, and he grabbed my forearm like a man about to plummet from a tall building. "Tell them to go away," he pleaded, his desperate eyes filled with tears. "Tell them to go away!"

I couldn't understand why he was so upset. I turned toward the opening just in time to see Elizabeth, now filled with absolute joy, disappear into the pulsing light.

"Come on, let's go!" I cried, wanting desperately to follow her. But the old man only gripped my arm more tightly. He was terrified, but why? The voices from the light had started again. I could hear their low, murmuring call of ultimate love. What was he hearing? What could he possibly be so afraid of?

The man sobbed. An awful croaking sound blocked his throat. "Why can't they just leave me alone? Why do they keep coming?"

"Who?" I said urgently. "Who are you so afraid of?"

"I don't want to go to hell," he cried. "I want to stay here."

His answer knocked me backward. "Hell! What are you talking about?"

"That's the only other place there is. If I'm not here, I'll go straight to hell!" Through his wrenching sobs, he reproached himself. "Why didn't I change in time? Why didn't I pay attention to the Bible while I still had a chance?"

I leaned over his face and spoke as gently as I knew how, "There is no hell. You're not going there, and neither is anyone else. That's your soul calling to you."

"But," he continued to punish himself, "I don't deserve anything but hell. I should have paid attention to the preacher. He told me I would end up this way if I didn't come back to church," He pleaded, "Make them go away. Please, please make them go away."

The light from the doorway had increased and now washed over us in splendid profusion. The voice began to sing, each gentle note was so filled with love, "Come...come my dear one. Please come home..."

Stroking the old man's forehead, I looked deeply into his eyes. "That is your soul. Can't you hear her? She has no desire to punish you or take you to an awful place filled with judgment and retribution. That's all a terrible misunderstanding. Listen to me, I've been there. I've seen it. There's nothing to be afraid of. I don't know how you ended up with Joe, but you're in the wrong place. There's so much more waiting for you in the embrace of your soul."

"But the Bible..." he said weakly, now focusing all of his attention on my face.

"That's all mixed up," I replied. "People have distorted it to further their own power. Listen to your soul. Can you feel her love? That's what's real, not some convoluted, manipulative tradition of confusion."

Hope began to find a way into his heart, and his eyes widened. "The Bible is wrong?"

Taking a deep breath, I answered from my deepest heart, "Yes. Much of the Bible is wrong."

"Oh," he shuddered. "You're going to go to hell, too. You can't say things like that!"

"No," I said without fear. "No, I'm not. Creating terror by telling you that you'll go to hell if you question the Bible, or the church, is just another way for people to keep the power they have over others. Listen to me, the Bible doesn't even make sense if you allow yourself to think about it."

"It doesn't?" he whispered.

"No, it doesn't," I answered firmly. "Why would a loving God want to send you into eternal damnation? Why would he create a son just so that son could suffer and die in order to save the people from his anger? Why wouldn't he just love the people and help them?

"And Jesus?" he questioned cautiously, clearly thinking that this wonderful teacher was waiting to inflict punishment for his transgressions.

"Jesus was a true gift to humanity," I answered. "He tried to teach us about the beauty of the soul, and how to reach that soul.

But what Jesus said has been so totally mixed up, it doesn't reflect what he meant anymore."

"He isn't going to send me to hell?" the old man cried.

"No," I replied softly. "Of course not. Just go with your soul. You'll be perfectly all right, I promise." Seeing he wanted to trust me, I offered, "Here, let me help you up."

Gently, I lifted the crumpled, tired body from the ground. Wiping his tears away, I repeated, "It's all right, I promise. Just look at what waits for you."

The rays of silver now began to undulate like a beckoning hand. The singing voice grew louder, and waves of love swept over us. Dazzled, I helped the old man slowly limp toward his destiny. The sound of his soul began to wash away all of his fear. "Come now...come home...my precious one...come home."

Suddenly, one long, deep sob rose from deep within the man and he cried, "Oh...oh my God." A smile transformed his face into a beacon of joy.

Together, we went through the gateway and into another world.

Thirty Six

A brilliant pathway of golden light stretched out into the distance. Undulating, vibrating, it curved itself around us, and formed a glorious tunnel. Contained within that space, we were welcomed with a sense of complete peace and indescribable love. There was absolutely nothing to fear.

The old man's body began to shift its form. Gradually, his features softened and glowed as the light penetrated his being.

"Oh!" he suddenly cried. "There's Kathleen—my sister! I thought you were dead! Where have you been all this time?"

A woman had emerged from the light. She took the old man's left hand, while I continued to hold his right. Her face was luminous with love, and she extended her arm to indicate the way.

A gentle melody wrapped around us, and the light grew even brighter. As we went forward, the old man continued to greet people he had known during his lifetime. Each one joined with him as we steadily journeyed toward the unknown.

As though we were heading straight into the sun, we continued on our way. Each time I thought our surroundings couldn't possibly become any more beautiful, they intensified. The old man's physical features were all but gone. They had been replaced by threads of spinning light that had assumed a beautiful new form. At his center, a ball of condensed light slowly turned. Inside that ball, particles of light struggled to float, but they seemed to be weighed down by a sticky, brown substance.

Suddenly, I heard the soft voice of a woman. Her words wrapped around the melody, and she sang, "Come to me. Come my beautiful creation. Bring all that you are most ashamed of. Do not hide yourself any longer. Bring forth your ugliest. Give all of it to me. For when it is all brought into the shower of God, it is made clean and new again. Offer all of it to me. I am here, and you are most loved."

The ball inside the man responded to her words. The energy inside it vibrated and grew brighter.

The woman continued her sweet song, "The way you become perfect and beautiful is to throw open your heart and say 'Here I am, here I am. Though I am dirty and broken and confused, take me into your arms where I belong. Clean me and soothe me, love me.'"

The ball inside the man surged forward in joy and began to spin rapidly, filling with the bright gold that surrounded us. As I watched, the glowing threads released themselves from the form and like incandescent yarn wound back into a ball, those threads disappeared into the ball of light at his center. All that remained of the old man was his now beautiful heart.

The friends who had accompanied us suddenly lost their forms and the spinning balls that were their hearts shot forward out of our sight.

Now, we were only two spinning spheres of magnificent beauty, barely discernible from the light of the pathway. Faster and faster we went toward something that pulsed with a deep, resonate throb. An incredible desire to join with that sound rose within me. I felt that I must be only a few feet away from a cherished lover. I couldn't bear to be separated one moment longer.

The throbbing became a steady heartbeat, and the song of the woman became like a glorious lullaby. "Come to me, my beautiful creation. Come to me." Now the woman appeared before us. Exquisitely beautiful, her own heart spun so rapidly, it appeared to be perfectly still. Reaching out her arms, she cried, "Oh my dear one, you are home."

The old man's heart leaped forward in a final surge of triumphant joy, and he disappeared straight into the heart of his soul.

She turned her attention to me and said, "You see, there is no need to grieve over the death of the physical body. I hold this one in my deepest heart. I welcome him as my precious servant. His battered mind is now only filled with my love; his shattered body has been made whole with the energies of my devotion.

"I have always whispered to him. At last, he hears my praise, my gratitude, my dismissal of all things he had seen as unforgivable. There is no thing which is unforgivable in my eyes. All confusion, all fear has been washed away with the tears of our glorious reunion.

"I will sing the lullaby of forever to my love and rock him softly. Here, he knows that there is no separation except that which is made by confusion and misunderstanding. There is no end except to despair, there is no end except to uncertainty, there is no end except to fear.

"He is my creation, my perfect issue. I welcome my sweet child back into the endless tides of creation and divine passion. He is now pure love. That is how I made him and that is what he has returned to be.

"At last...at last...he is home."

Can you see love? How do you know it's there? How do you know that you love someone or that they love you? It cannot be measured. You just know. Why didn't we honor spirit in the same way that we did love? Why weren't we ever allowed to say, "I just know" when it came to the soul?

Thirty Seven

"Hello there!" Daniel's voice drifted toward me.

"Daniel?" I struggled to rouse myself from the hypnotic beauty of my experience with the old man's soul. Looking around, I could see that my environment had changed dramatically. Tall pine trees surrounded me as I sat on a boulder. Wonderful, warm sunshine played across my arms, and I was filled with deep contentment.

He came into view. "Death isn't the way many people think it will be, is it?" he asked, a smile broad on his face.

"No," I answered softly.

Daniel gracefully climbed up on the boulder, and sat beside me, his hand resting on my knee.

"Where are we?" I felt obliged to ask, but I really didn't care anymore.

"On Earth," he answered simply. "I thought we'd visit ordinary reality for a while."

Ordinary reality. What a sad thing it was. We were all so profoundly limited when we relied only on the things we could perceive with our senses. Daniel had once told me, "invisible doesn't equal imaginary." Why did we insist that it did? We were so afraid to trust anything we couldn't measure, but what I had experienced was impossible to count and weigh.

Can you see love? How do you know it's there? How do you know that you love someone or that they love you? It cannot be measured. You just know. Why didn't we honor spirit in the same way that we did love? Why weren't we ever allowed to say, "I just know" when it came to the soul? Immediately, the harsh statements would begin, "Nobody knows for sure that God even exists," "It's never been proven that there is such a thing as a soul," "No one can scientifically verify that life after death exists." Why couldn't we allow ourselves to perceive such things with our hearts and not with our judging, critical minds?

I thought about a dear friend of mine who had nearly died. After being resuscitated, she had awakened so filled with love and hope. Her doctor immediately discounted her experiences by mumbling about dying brain cells and synaptic misfires. Why couldn't he just listen and accept that something astounding had happened?

It must have to do with trust. We just do not trust each other. When someone reports a brush with the divine, we start looking for the possibility that he or she is taking us for a fool. We're afraid of what we cannot prove, and that fear makes it nearly impossible for spirit to be heard.

I took in a deep breath and readied myself to hear more about the things I couldn't usually see. Seeing that I was eager to listen, Daniel plunged right in. "You know, the old man had already lost his physical body when you met him."

"Oh, god." Maybe I wasn't so ready to hear more, after all. But without my permission, my mind raced along with a million questions. "Where were we? If he was dead, why wasn't he with his soul? "

"Wait. Wait!" Daniel chuckled.

"I have a lot of questions, Daniel!" I replied, feeling a touch defensive. "Just when I think I understand something, you blow me out of the water."

"That's how you learn, Karen!" he teased. "You see, the old man was what is called an entity."

"An entity? What's that?"

"Just a simple term for a very unfortunate being," he replied. "Sometimes a confused person who has lost his own physical body gets caught in the energy field of a living human being."

I brought up the only reference point I had for the idea that the dead could linger after the death of the body. "You mean like a haunted house?"

"To use your term, there are many more haunted people than there are haunted places on Earth."

Growing up on campfire stories of creepy ghosts creaking through old houses, I had plenty of room for the idea that dead people could somehow get stuck on Earth. But I never heard anyone talk about them getting tangled up with living human beings. "How can that be?" I exclaimed.

Opening his hands, he held a bubble. Inside it, brown, cloudy energy shifted clumsily back and forth. But I was horrified to see that something was struggling inside it.

A tiny, desperate man.

Daniel looked very sad. "The choice to stay with his social mind is a result of the person's unfamiliarity with the energies of the soul while he is on Earth. That's one of the reasons it's very important for the person to work to remove any obstructions between himself and his soul. Otherwise, upon death, his social mind will feel familiar and safe. The soul will feel like a stranger."

Thirty Eight

"Daniel!" I cried. "Who is that? We have to help him. Let him out of there!"

"You know what this is, Karen!" Daniel chided me gently, now lifting the bubble high into the air.

It could only be one thing. "That's some poor human being caught in his social mind!" As I watched the bubble, I could see glorious, shimmering energy surrounding it. It sparkled, danced, and glowed in constant movement around the bubble.

Daniel shifted his hands a little, and the glorious light seemed to multiply itself, now growing so large it surrounded us both. But the tiny man inside kept struggling, oblivious to its presence.

"I wish the soul would just blow that capsule apart," I said fervently. But I knew it had to respect free will.

"Why are you showing me this social mind? What does it have to do with entities?"

"An entity is an intact social mind whose body has ceased to be." He watched me try to grasp what he had said.

"The social mind can continue to exist, even without a body?" I croaked, unsure I wanted to know about this.

As usual, Daniel didn't rescue me, but simply announced, "Indeed."

This wasn't easy information to take. "So, the social mind can wander around after death!"

He replied calmly. "It can."

I tried to put the pieces of my limited understanding together. "But, since it's not connected with its soul, it doesn't have any energy supply of its own, does it?"

"No," he agreed. "That's why it has to find the energy of a living person in order to sustain itself."

I struggled to accept the frightening information, and then said, "The old man said he was inside somebody called Joe Delario. At least I think that's what his name was. Who's Joe Delario?"

"That's not important." Daniel answered. "All you need to understand right now is that he was alive on the Earth."

"But Joe had the old man inside of him?"

"Not in his physical body, but inside his energy field."

I was outraged on behalf of this unsuspecting stranger. "So entities are just social minds floating around out there waiting to feed off of some poor living person? But I thought a person's social mind automatically ended when their body ended."

"Only when the soul is allowed to burn it away," he replied.

This was all so different from anything I had been taught about death. I had accepted the Methodist 'blip off to heaven' concept. You die; you end up in heaven. There are no complications to consider. "My God, are you telling me that a person can choose to stay within his own social mind, rather than return to their soul?"

Daniel looked very sad. "The choice to stay with his social mind is a result of the person's unfamiliarity with the energies of the soul while he is on Earth. That's one of the reasons it's very important for the person to work to remove any obstructions between himself and his soul. Otherwise, upon death, his social mind will feel familiar and safe. The soul will feel like a stranger."

As I stared at him, he added, "Even someone like Elizabeth can become confused."

"Elizabeth!" I cried. "Elizabeth was dead. But she had no idea! She thought she was on her way to meet her daughter!"

"She was a lost entity. You see, her body was destroyed in a sudden car crash. She had no time to realize she was about to die. She didn't have any chance to adjust."

"But where was her soul?" I asked, feeling sick. "Surely, someone like Elizabeth would know to go right into the arms of her soul!"

"That is where religious confusion takes a terrible toll," he answered. "You see, she was taught to expect an enormous choir of angels to meet her after death."

This was mind-boggling! Confused, I finally sputtered, "What did she see?"

"She saw the bright light of her own soul and felt its compelling love. However, it wasn't enough for her to overcome the grief-stricken calls of her daughter. Elizabeth succumbed to the concerns of the Earth. She felt the unwillingness of those who were close to her to let her go. Their grief was very understandable, given the confusion which exists about the death of the body. She turned to follow their longing. Once she went back toward the direction of Earth, she quickly became disoriented."

The beautiful meadow Elizabeth and I wandered into must have been Joe's energy field. She had felt so much better; she had just wanted to sit down and stay there. I asked tentatively, "Elizabeth might have stopped looking for her own soul and stayed with Joe, right?"

"Possibly," Daniel replied. "But we would have continued to come and offer her a return home. Perhaps one day, she would have finally accepted."

Mulling these amazing ideas over for a while, I finally asked, "But what about Joe? Having these other people in his energy field couldn't be good for him. Gosh, I wouldn't want that old man hanging around me for very long!"

Daniel looked at me for a few moments, as if he was trying to decide something. Then he said, "Let's go back in time. I'll show you exactly what the old man was doing to Joe."

*Glancing around me, I tried to determine
where I had landed this time. Sitting on either
side of a wide, oak dining table, a man and
woman were in the midst of an argument.
Oblivious to my presence, they glared at
one another.*

♥

Thirty Nine

"I don't like your attitude!" The woman's voice was sharp and bitter. Glancing around me, I tried to determine where I had landed this time. Sitting on either side of a wide, oak dining table, a man and woman were in the midst of an argument. Oblivious to my presence, they glared at one another.

"What do you mean by that?" The man responded to her critical attack.

"What's gotten into you lately? You seem so angry all the time," she shot back.

"You're exaggerating, as usual," he said wearily. "I'm just worn out, that's all. Get off my back."

"Well, go to a doctor."

"I'm not sick, just under a lot of pressure," the man replied. "And I'm sorry if I seem angry. I'm not angry at you at all."

"What about the other night?"

"The other night?"

Face contorted with anger; she snapped at him. "Don't tell me you don't remember! Come on, take responsibility for what you say."

The man was obviously confused. "What are you talking about?"

The woman had started to cry. "When I didn't want to make love the other night, you called me a bitch. Don't think I didn't hear you!"

"I didn't mean that! You know me better. I don't know where that came from."

"Well, you said it," she croaked. "It hurt me a lot, Joe."

Joe? I must be in Joe's house. What was I doing here? I couldn't see his soul anymore, just an ordinary, middle-class home. Obviously, Joe and his wife had no idea I had intruded on their privacy. What was the point of me being here?

"I didn't want to make love because I don't like the way you've been touching me lately. You're so rough and always in a hurry. You've never been like that. What's going on?"

"I don't know, Emily. I don't know." Joe muttered.

"Well, you'd better figure it out!" his wife cried. "You don't seem like yourself at all. You had another nightmare, didn't you?"

He sighed, "Yeah, I did. Same one. An old man is yelling at me, trying to get me to do something I don't want to do. I don't even know what it is. He's screaming away and I can't fix it because I don't even know what he wants."

"Please go to a doctor, Joe," she pleaded. "Or maybe you should see a counselor. Something's bothering you. We have to find out what it is."

Suddenly, Joe jumped up and pointed his finger at Emily. His voice splintering with rage, he yelled, "Don't you speak to me that way! Don't you ever tell me what to do!"

Overcome by tears, his wife fled the room, the door slamming a loud goodbye.

And I found myself staring into Daniel's blue eyes.

Forty

"**D**aniel!" I cried. "Joe's life was being ruined! He didn't even know what was happening to him. He had no idea the old man was in his energy field!"

I thought to look around to see where we might be. Now on a sheet of violet light, a bright doorway lay far off in the distance. I almost asked him about the specifics of our location but thought better of it. What difference did it make? He was going to propel me into every situation he thought I needed. I might as well just accept it.

"Why doesn't anybody ever talk about that phenomenon? It seems terribly important!"

But I already knew why the subject of entities never came up. We would all have to accept a lot of things which were contrary to the religion of science that we all bowed down to. We would have to talk about things like the fact that a human being is an energy field and not just flesh and bones. We would have to bring up the most taboo topic in western culture—death.

We hated death. We were frightened about it, and we didn't understand it. Our priests and ministers spoke eloquently at funerals, but nobody really believed what they had to say...at least not enough to quit being afraid. No one could prove that anybody survives after death and so, it was mysterious and scary.

"Daniel," I queried. "What was happening with Joe seemed so unfair. He had no idea that the old man had invaded his space, and neither did Emily. Their marriage could have been destroyed by that entity, and they would have never known the real reason for it!"

"It happens to many people on the Earth," he replied, setting off an alarm within me.

"And nobody knows!" I cried. "Depending on the character of the entity, I suppose all kinds of results are possible."

"Indeed," Daniel said somberly. "The old man knew he was dead and that he was living in Joe's energy field."

"He even knew he was having a negative effect on him," I exclaimed. "But he didn't care at all. His only concern was for himself."

"That is frequently the case with this type of entity," Daniel replied.

"Type?" I said lamely. Apparently, entities differed somehow from one another.

"Elizabeth was a lost entity," he explained. "The old man wasn't lost, at all. Certain entities know exactly where they are and what they are doing. However, they are terribly confused about what their alternatives are. The old man was so afraid of spirit he thought his only chance to survive was to stay with Joe. He didn't care if he hurt him, but he didn't intend to do that."

"So, he wasn't malicious," I sighed. "Just selfish."

"Just confused," Daniel replied patiently. "It is always a violation when anyone except the rightful owner tries to live within one's energy field. Joe's energy body was meant only for him. It couldn't truly support anyone else."

"I saw what the effects of the old man were on Joe. But what about Elizabeth? What would have happened to him if she had stayed there?

"Probably Joe would have simply felt tired and sad after a while. He might have gone to his doctor, thinking something was physically wrong. The doctor would find nothing and send Joe off thinking he had an emotional problem."

I had certainly had an enormous number of clients over the years who came on the recommendation of a physician. They had sat in my office expressing frustration about mysterious symptoms. Often, they had been fine one day, and suddenly very tired the next. After trying vitamins, a different diet, more exercise, and more rest, they came to me at the end of their rope. Being a diligent therapist, I had labored to find an emotional reason for their physical problems.

Stress was always a good explanation. But with so many patients, even when we had altered their entire life to reduce their stress, even when we had ferreted out all possible contributors and made adjustments accordingly, so often they felt the exact way they had when they entered into therapy. It had been terribly frustrating for both of us. Usually, they thanked me for my help and went off to explore yet another method of treatment.

"And consider what happens when an energy body is asked to supply enough for three beings, or four or eight," Daniel broke in.

"Oh my God," I cried. "I would think the person would eventually be unable to do much of anything at all."

"There are many fortunate cultures on your Earth that understand about the existence of entities. When there's a sudden change in a person's health or personality, spiritual interference is the very first thing that is looked for. But in America, that knowledge has been ridiculed, and all but lost. Many, many people suffer as a consequence."

Something amazing occurred to me. "Daniel, do entities have anything to do with mental illness?"

"Many people whom you call mentally ill have nothing wrong with them, at all. They are having true, positive encounters with the divine. Your culture doesn't accept spirit and so, it cannot accept that anyone could have experiences with spirit. The social mind, in the form of various professionals, rises up and tries to stamp out those experiences as rapidly as possible."

I knew from my experiences with Daniel how incredibly hard it was to convince people that it was possible to hear the voice of spirit. I was painfully aware that some of my friends were convinced I had suffered a breakdown.

Daniel interrupted my thoughts. "Why is it that people are allowed to talk to God, but when they hear an answer, they're considered to be crazy?"

I laughed and said, "I never thought about it like that! But I've worked with many people in my own counseling practice who were plagued by voices that urged them toward violence and encouraged self-hatred. What about that, Daniel?"

"Painful and destructive experiences do not come from the soul. There are many possible causes, including chemical imbalances, emotional trauma, and family dynamics, to name only a few. But, sometimes, those experiences are the result of entity interference. Some entities are quite capable of entering into the sensory field of a living person. They can produce terrible hallucinations and nightmares. The voices can urge a living person to do all sorts of things he or she doesn't really want to do. An entity can even masquerade as the voice of God or pretend to be an angel. That's why it's so important that people understand that naively calling out to anything in the universe to come to them is dangerous."

I thought immediately of many well-publicized murder cases. Often, a person who committed a terrible crime reported hearing voices that told him to do it. Maybe those people really were coerced by something the rest of us couldn't hear, see, or believe in. Of course, that didn't release the person from his responsibility for what he had done. But it lent a whole new understanding to the phenomenon of 'senseless killings.' And, if an entity with terrible motives attached itself to a living person the result wasn't hard to imagine.

There were many books that promoted techniques to channel spirits or contact angels. It seemed all one had to do was open wide to the universe and all sorts of benevolent beings would swoop down and extend their wisdom. It had felt dangerous to me, somehow. Now I understood why.

"There are many beings without bodies surrounding your world," Daniel said quietly. "Most of them are far from wise. You know, your famous doctor, Carl Jung, knew about these things many years ago," Daniel said quietly. "He took them seriously and even tried to talk with the entities through his patients."

"He did?"

"Indeed. He was a brave man. His own contemporaries grew wary of him because he refused to simply ignore his patients' experiences in favor of 'science.' But I must remind you, there are many, many cultures on your Earth who acknowledge the existence of entities without question. I'm afraid their 'patients' fare much better than do yours."

We really could be an arrogant people at times. We were so sure that our concepts and beliefs were right; we often completely ignored any evidence to the contrary. Our mental health system was one manifestation of that arrogance. Instead of examining why we couldn't see and hear those things outside of ordinary sensory reality, we insisted that anyone who did must get back inside the boundaries that we defined.

I laughed a little as I suddenly thought about how Louis Pasteur must have been greeted when he tried to tell people that illness was caused by tiny invisible germs. It wasn't acceptable when he said it, but ultimately, it turned out to be true. Maybe the existence of entities and their effects on mental health would someday be accepted as obvious. "Tell me," I said urgently. "What do we do to prevent entities from invading our space?"

"You must always keep your energy strong," he replied. "That's the real reason behind the religious teaching about what to eat and how to behave. It doesn't have to do with pleasing God. It's about keeping your energy strong."

"You mean like saying we shouldn't drink, smoke or eat pork... that kind of thing?" I grew up in the Methodist church where there were almost no prohibitions of any kind. But I had friends from different denominations who were armed with a whole list of "Don't do's." And Daniel was right; they said the reason to follow those rules was to please God and prevent his wrath. But Daniel was saying that many of the activities we called 'sins' were just things which would weaken our energy fields.

Daniel continued. "When you use alcohol or drugs, the periphery of your energy field is weakened. Anesthesia and negative places like bars, hospitals, or prisons can do the same thing. Over time, even relentlessly antagonistic people can shred your protection. A blow to the head or any injury creates an opening in your protection, as can long-term emotional distress."

I considered what he had said. My own intuition had told me this information a long time ago. I just never paid attention. Certain places and people left me feeling weak and uneasy. I naturally avoided those things which undermined my energy. I thought about a potential experiment. If you blindfolded someone and took him into a jail, he probably would be able sense that he was in negative surroundings. Even if we didn't accept the idea of an energy field, some places felt good, and some didn't.

I had so many thoughts multiplying in my head; I could hardly choose which question to ask. "One thing really bothers me about this. What about the issue of self-responsibility? We can't go around blaming everything on negative spiritual influences!"

"Of course not," Daniel replied. "Once you know about entity interference, you have to accept more responsibility for yourself, not less."

"How do we do that?"

"You can make consistent, healthy choices to keep your energy strong," he answered. "You can watch for the warning signs of entity interference."

"What are they?" I asked urgently.

He seemed pleased about my earnest desire to know. "An abrupt change in personality, a sudden interest in abusing alcohol or drugs, rage attacks without a previous history of having them."

"What else?"

"A precipitous loss of energy without medical cause, as well as other sudden and unexplained physical problems. Uncharacteristic behaviors."

"Like Joe's problems with Emily?" I asked.

"Indeed. You must understand that I am saying that it's important to include the possibility of spiritual interference. I am not saying that every problem or symptom is the result of entity attachment. But by totally excluding that phenomenon, many people suffer without anyone understanding what's happening to them."

Something horrifying occurred to me. "Daniel, if an entity attaches to your energy field, are you stuck with it forever?"

"Of course not," he said reassuringly. "Other cultures have practitioners that can help to release the entity. Fortunately, your country is starting to have some of them, too. Often, you can push an entity away by yourself by strengthening your energy field and directing your concentration and intent."

"That's a relief," I said with a sigh.

Almost immediately, Daniel robbed me of my security. "I have only shown you two types of entities, Karen. You're not quite ready to learn about the rest."

His judgment about my readiness was so correct, I didn't need to respond. The sooner I forgot about what he had only hinted at, the more comfortable I would be. I went swiftly to a safer question. "Daniel, do a lot of us miss our chance to be with our own soul when we die?"

"Too many," he said, sounding very sad. "Unfortunately, your religions nurture the illusion that you're not good enough for God.

Many of you secretly believe that you're not worthy to accept the love that you are offered. You might even feel that you're nothing, but a collection of failures. When you die, you're afraid to let go because you're convinced you couldn't possibly deserve to be loved. But you see God's heart is much bigger than yours. Don't judge the capacities of spirit by your simple, limited social mind."

"Just like that old man was convinced he was going to hell," I said. But, as I had just seen, the man's soul had not judged him, counted his wrongs and rights, or measured his worthiness. She had simply welcomed him home.

"In your culture, death is a very confused thing," Daniel said. He walked toward the brilliant light shining from the distant doorway. "Come, I will show you."

Forty One

As soon as I crossed the threshold of the doorway, I began to fall. Terrified, I clutched madly at invisible walls and desperately tried to save myself. Blazing yellow light went by at an incredible speed. Battling hysteria, and hardly able to breathe, I plummeted like an elevator unleashed from its tether of steel.

I had always been afraid of falling from a great height. Everybody is. It would mean certain death. That thought brought a surprising sense of calm. After all, I couldn't really die in this place. This was the realm of spirit. If I died, I would only end up right back here!

With that realization, my fall abruptly stopped. I heard Daniel say, "You see, Karen, death is not really very important at all...that is, if you know who you truly are."

A stark hospital room suddenly appeared. Sterile, unadorned, it smelled of urine and medicinal alcohol. A single light sent a violent message from its position over the bed. Dangling from the bed rail, a crucifix swayed, its motion copying the rolling movement of the frail woman on the mattress.

"I'm so afraid," she moaned. "Don't let me die. Please, don't let me die." In awful pain, she moved constantly as though trying to escape the point of a dagger.

"Trust in God, my dear." The priest by her side was dressed in black. His voice was low and confident. He tried to interrupt her fear.

"But my sins father. I have so many sins," she murmured pitifully. Cold sweat ran down her face.

A puffy white hand patted her emaciated arm. "I have absolved you from all of your sins, my dear," the priest said comfortably.

The woman sobbed, "Oh father...how do you know? How do you know I will not be punished in the fire forever?"

"The church has dealt with sin from the time our Savior appeared to save us all. If you repent and accept him, you will be saved." He recited the words without feeling. Clearly, he had said the same thing over a thousand bedsides. Did he believe it himself?

"But I have done so many things I shouldn't have!" the woman cried. "I knew they were sins, and I did them any way. Are you sure you truly have the power to remove the darkness from my soul?"

"Of course," he asserted, a careful yawn hiding behind his fingers. "There is nothing to be frightened of as long as you accept Jesus and the authority of the church."

The woman was begging for intimacy at the hour of her death, but the priest hid comfortably behind a well-practiced performance. It suddenly seemed so perfectly symbolic to me. How many truly intimate encounters do we allow ourselves to have during our lifetime? So much of what we do involves figuring out what to say and how to be in order to stay safely hidden behind a wall of emotional deception. We don't want anyone to recognize who we think we are. Most of our time is spent in an awful game of dodging and darting so that no one will ever know the shame-filled secrets we hold deep inside.

And, like this poor woman, most of us will maintain our isolation until we cease to breathe. What is the point of all that? Without an awareness of the presence of her soul, without a clear connection to that soul, she could only look to an outside authority to give her comfort.

That's what I was seeing in this macabre dance between the dying woman and the unavailable priest. He had no more connection to his own soul than she did. During her last minutes on

Earth, she was trying to break through her entrapment, and he had nothing to offer but rhetoric. He couldn't afford to be intimate with her. There was nothing behind his mask. She knew it and so did he, but neither one of them could afford to say anything. Desperately trying to assuage her fear, she needed him to really know what he did not. He sat waiting for her to die. If she would just give up, he would never be exposed.

I cried for her and for all of us. What a terrible way to end life on Earth! I wanted to hold her in my arms and tell of all the things I had seen. But she could not see or hear me. For the first time, I experienced a taste of what the soul must feel while watching a human being suffer. Because of free will, if the suffering person stayed locked within her social mind, the soul couldn't get through to offer its love.

Suddenly pulled backwards, I traveled rapidly down a long radiant tunnel. Shooting out the end of it, I landed in another room. An old man sat upright in his bed. A colorful quilt of red and blue lay over him. This room was filled with plants and bright pictures. Beautiful sunlight filtered through lace curtains. A big orange cat snuggled luxuriously up against the man's leg.

"Hello, Henry," a nurse said brightly as she entered the room. "I've brought your medicine."

"Oh good, Anna," he replied. "I haven't had a spot of pain since I got here, and I don't want to start now."

Carefully, she prepared his arm and injected his medication. He smiled at her and remained alert and talkative. I had never seen anything like that. The clients I had visited in the hospital were always foggy or nearly unconscious after a serious pain medication had been given. The nurse had arrived before he had suffered a hint of discomfort. That was different, too. Usually, physicians were so afraid of contributing to an addiction; they limited drug administration until the very last minute. The patient was often reduced to screaming and begging for relief.

"You know," the old man said quietly. "I do think I will be leaving this evening."

"Really, Henry?" the nurse said, looking deep into his eyes. "I'm so glad I had a chance to see you."

"Thank you for your help," he replied. "I do appreciate all your kindness. Gladys will take Miss Kitty home for me."

"You're very welcome, Henry," Anna said kindly. "It has been a pleasure. Can we do anything more for you? Would you like some company?"

"No," he responded, a slow grin crossing his face. "I believe I have everything I need."

"All right, then," the nurse replied, holding his hand for a moment. "If you change your mind, just give a call and I'll come right away."

Where was he going? He didn't look like he was in any condition to return home. Perhaps he was being transferred to another hospital. I was amazed at how alert and comfortable he continued to be. What kind of medicine had he been given? And the cat! What hospital would allow a cat to come through its doors, let alone lay on a patient's bed?

Anna left the room, a smile sent over her shoulder. "Well, now," the man whispered, "exactly how do I do this? Where do we go from here?" Who was he talking to? Perhaps Miss Kitty... but Henry was looking away from the cat. She continued to sleep, her soft breath rising and falling with complete comfort.

"Would you like to wait to see Gladys once more?" The gentle, sweet voice was followed by the appearance of a glorious being of light. Sitting on his bed, her form was filled with moving effervescent beads of silver and gold. She held his worn hand in hers and stroked his forehead with deep love. Her clear blue eyes never left his.

"No, I don't believe I want to wait. It's time to go," he said with certainty. Without a trace of fear, he had welcomed her presence as though she was a beloved friend.

"All right," she said, carefully gathering the man in her arms. "Just hold on to me. That's right. Now, just come right through your heart."

As I watched, a shimmering wave of silver and gold colored light began to move upward from Henry's feet and hands. It went through his legs and abdomen and continued up his chest. Then energy from his head began to flow down through his neck and into the chest. As the energy was withdrawn, his body became absolutely still and dark.

Now, sparkling particles of energy inside his heart formed a glowing, beautiful pulsing ball of golden and silver light. And finally, as the energy tightened into a smaller and smaller ball, it simply rolled out of his heart away from his physical form. Once free, the energy which had animated the man streamed joyfully into the heart of his soul.

Overcome by the beauty of what I had just seen, I closed my tear-filled eyes and bowed my head in thanks. A gentle touch on my shoulder roused my attention and I glanced up to find Henry's soul looking lovingly into my eyes.

"Come with me," she said softly. "I want you to see something."

"Human life is most precious," she said passionately. "The body should be helped to heal when it has been injured or is suffering with an unnecessary disease process. But, when it cannot be restored to something useful for its owner, it is time to leave. There is no question that the spirit that inhabits that body will receive another vehicle at the appropriate time."

Forty Two

Instantly, we were in the realm of the first heaven. Henry's soul had taken my hand and now led me across the expanse of rainbow light.

"What I saw you do with Henry was so beautiful," I whispered.

"Henry was a person who was very familiar with me," she replied happily. "He lived most of his life in his natural mind, so he could hear me and often see me. He had escaped from his own social mind very early. He knew there was no true separation between us. So, coming back into my heart seemed completely natural to him. You could see that he had no fear of death, at all. "

"I know! That was an amazing thing to watch," I exclaimed. "He was so calm, and free of pain."

"Unfortunately, the disintegration of the physical body often involves pain," she said. "But there are many places on Earth where doctors are not afraid to administer appropriate pain medications. Medical science knows how to completely alleviate discomfort, but physicians are often unwilling to offer what works. In America, many substances are not available to the doctors, even if they want to use them to help their patients."

I thought about how comfortable Henry's surroundings had been. "He wasn't in a hospital, was he?"

"Not in the ordinary sense. Hospitals are often an example of the social mind at work. They have many rules and many methods by which to control the feelings and perceptions of both the staff and the patients."

My heart stirred with compassion. "But why?"

"Hospitals are based on a terrible fear of death," she answered. "The social mind does not want to face its demise. It knows that its existence is false and that it faces extinction. Your culture does everything it can to avoid thinking about death because most people have no connection to their soul. Hospitals control reality by hiding people who are dying. They make the environment as different as possible from everyday life. That way, people can put those who are dying into a different category than themselves. They can avoid looking at the fact that they will eventually die, too."

"So, hospitals depersonalize death to protect us from thinking about our own, inevitable end."

"Like the woman you saw with her priest, most of you are deeply afraid of death. You avoid thinking about it for most of your life. When it finally appears to be inevitable, you look to authorities to comfort you. But you know they don't have any personal experience with the afterlife, so they cannot really offer reassurance. Unfortunately, most of you die from within the perspective of your social mind. You are deeply afraid and feel you are losing all that you thought was 'you.'"

Suddenly, I thought about the countless bugs I had washed down the drain of my shower. I had found them lurking behind the shower curtain and had quickly turned the water on them full blast. Soon, they'd scoot toward the drain, unable to save themselves. Circling that dark hole, eventually they would disappear into it. Most of us felt that death was like that. We couldn't stop it, and it seemed terrifying.

Henry's nurse had accepted the fact that he was about to die. "The place that Henry was in accepted death and acknowledged his experience without fear."

"Indeed," she replied. "In fact, his surroundings encouraged him to let go of the physical body. This was possible because everyone there already had familiarity with the energies of the soul. They knew there was nothing to fear, not because of stalwart religious beliefs, but because they actually had experience with what comes after death."

"I bet there weren't any heroic efforts to save the body in that place!" I exclaimed.

"Of course not. Why work desperately to preserve something that no longer serves the soul or the person that soul sent to the Earth? When your automobile becomes obsolete, you do not connect it to machines to keep it going. It has lost its usefulness."

"That's an interesting perspective."

"Human life is most precious," she said passionately. "The body should be helped to heal when it has been injured or is suffering with an unnecessary disease process. But, when it cannot be restored to something useful for its owner, it is time to leave. There is no question that the spirit that inhabits that body will receive another vehicle at the appropriate time."

"Do we all come back to live another life on the Earth?" For some reason, I was still resisting that idea.

She laughed. "I think it was Voltaire who said, 'After all, it is no more surprising to be born twice than is to be born once.' Most human beings are nowhere near the point in their learning process to leave the Earth school behind. It is very safe to assume that you will be returning. Usually, there is about a one hundred year interval between lifetimes."

"Why so long?"

"That is a very short period of time from the perspective of spirit," she replied. "There are many experiences that need to be absorbed by the soul between lifetimes. It is important to use those experiences to further our growth."

I took in a big breath, "Henry was a very unusual person. He had such intimate contact with you for most of his years. What was his life like?"

The soul's smile sparkled with joy. "He knew my constant love and devotion. Unlike so many people, he was never confused about his purpose for being on the Earth. Very early in his life, he knew what occupation would match that purpose. He was able to ask for my help whenever he had an important decision to make. His nature spirit was nurtured and appreciated. Consequently, his body was vigorous and strong. When his mate came along, he knew who she was immediately. They created a wonderful, loving, spiritually based relationship together. He didn't waste effort over the concerns of the social mind and was able to offer boundless acceptance and love to those around him. On those few occasions when he had a true need to protect himself, he met the challenge with the certainty that he had more than enough strength to do it. And, he never had a moment's fear of death."

"That's the way it's supposed to be for all of us," I breathed. "Life on Earth could be so different."

"Henry also had a very clean heart," the soul said happily. "That made living a great joy."

I looked over at her and felt confused. "What do you mean he had a clean heart?"

"Oh," she said, clearly surprised at my question. "I thought Daniel had told you all about that."

"No. He never said anything about it."

"Well," she smiled. "I guess it's up to me to show you." With that, Henry's soul slowly faded into the light.

Involuntarily, I braced for the unexpected. In the blink of an eye, I was transported to another place.

Forty Three

As usual, I didn't have a clue about where I might be. A thick fog surrounded me on all sides. I took a few, tentative steps forward, but I quickly discovered that moving anywhere was useless. The air seemed heavy, and I could see no farther than a few feet ahead of me.

Then, I heard a low, moaning voice rumbling off in the distance, and the fog began to swirl in a dizzying frenzy. The moan surged into a deep wail, a sound I had only heard when people grieved. Suddenly, the fog parted, and I could see for miles. Far away, a wall of darkness seemed to rise up from the ground. As I watched, it grew taller and taller. Now gaining speed, it rushed toward me like a tidal wave in a frightening dream. Trying to flee, my feet were gummed to an invisible floor. I screamed; certain the wave would cancel my existence in one momentous crash. I crumpled down and waited for the inevitable.

"Karen, it's important to see." The quiet words were of no comfort and only rebounded through my terrified brain.

The air rushed by me, sucked into the massive black wave. "Daniel!" I cried. Every cell in my body begged for mercy.

Only twenty feet away, the wave abruptly stopped. I looked up at it and was shocked to see the faces of a thousand people. Many were crying, others paced frantically back and forth.

Abruptly, an enraged warrior jumped out of the wave and headed straight toward me. His eyes were surrounded by white paint, and his body was covered in red and orange. Striped feathers stuck straight out from his hair, and his face was contorted with the desire to kill.

My mind commanded me to protect myself, but there was

no place to hide. My eyes landed on the spear he clenched in his hands. I had known the agony of such a weapon before. I tried to flatten myself into the non-existent floor. As quickly as he had come, the warrior disappeared.

Confused, I gazed into the wave again and saw a city street. Young men hollered from battered cars with roaring engines. One snarled, "There he is." The statement carried an ominous promise of violence. Shots splintered the air, and I saw a child fall. There was no remorse here—only a gunned motor under the control of a frozen heart.

Oh, God. Why? Why? I silently cried. Concern for my own safety had been replaced with enormous grief.

Now I heard six people plotting to burn someone's home. Methodical, cold, they held no concern for anyone but themselves. Again, I pleaded to be taken away from this terrible place. Why had I been left here?

Suddenly, a shouting man stood over a woman. Horrified, I watched him hit her again and again, as she pleaded for mercy. I screamed for help, but no one came.

Scene after terrifying scene came forth from the wave. Men, women, even children seemed to be consumed with a desire to hurt other people. Finally, I couldn't deal with anything more and collapsed sobbing like a little child. With that, the wave vanished, and gentle arms lifted me up. Shuddering, I clutched the warmth of a strong shoulder and was carried off into the promise of freedom.

Forty Four

Exhausted, I was placed on a luminous field somewhere. Battered by the after effects of too much adrenaline, I was deeply grateful to be away from the wave. I decided to stand up, and my legs fought back. Rolling from side to side like someone on a boat in a storm, I changed my mind and sat down again. Instantly, Daniel appeared.

"Why did I have to see all that?" I asked weakly. "Couldn't the point have been made another way?"

"We had to break through your denial, Karen," he said without apology. "That's something humanity can no longer afford to exercise."

"Denial about what?" I asked a bit angrily. Nobody wants to hear they aren't facing something. Most of us like to protect the idea that we're courageous and willing to deal with life head on.

"You were shown the extreme results of a particular kind of energy—an energy that will cause humanity's ultimate destruction if something isn't done about it. It's easy for people to get caught up in the beauty of the spiritual world and forget about the work they have to do."

"You mean dismantling the social mind?"

"That social mind is responsible for contaminating the human heart."

A deep gray substance had come up out of the field of energy and now began to stick to my arms. There it congealed and clung to my fingers as I tried to wipe it off. "What is this stuff?"

"Just the kind of energy that can end up in someone's heart," he answered, watching as gooey matter began to cover the rest of my body.

I was quite frantic to free myself. Finally, I managed to fling some of the goop from my left hand. Sending it flying into the air, I said with disgust, "So, this is density. It's like tar—no wonder we can't see anything real when it's around!"

"If your windows were covered with this, would you be able to see anything outside?"

"No, I guess not," I said. I remembered that William Blake had said, "If the doors of perception were cleansed everything would appear to man as it is, infinite." His words had intrigued me when I had first read them. Now I really understood what he meant. We were literally being blocked by this ponderous form of energy from seeing what was truly important.

"The amount of density in your heart determines how you will think, feel, and behave."

Like most people, I had always thought our consciousness was determined by our mind. The more intelligent someone was, the higher his consciousness would be. But, after everything Daniel had shown me, I didn't believe that anymore. There were criminals in our midst who certainly didn't lack for intelligence. Some of our most simple citizens had an uncanny capacity for understanding the purest kinds of love.

"Wait a minute," I cried. "The soul's energy is supposed to flow into our hearts. If density's there, the compacted energy would occupy the space the soul is supposed to flow into!"

"Exactly," he said quietly.

I shook my head and asked, "But it's so ugly; why would anybody allow that to go on within themselves?"

Patiently, he continued, "Once the heart is clogged with density, the person forgets there can be anything else. He begins to see the world through that kind of heart. Soon, everything he sees only validates his own desperate condition."

"He can only see what his heart allows him to see," I exclaimed.

"That's why you once told me that people live in different worlds, depending on what kind of heart they have!"

"Precisely."

I considered the implications for a minute. "If you can't see anything but ugliness around you, then you think there aren't any alternatives. Your own thick heart can't perceive beauty, hope, or anything which isn't consistent with that heaviness inside."

"Then what happens, Karen?" he asked sadly.

"Then you act in accordance with what you perceive. If your own heart is filled with fear and violence, you see that around you. I suppose you could start to attract the same kind of energy into your life, because that's what you know how to deal with. You probably wouldn't even notice anything else."

"Remember, there are no bad hearts. But the level of density in a heart has destructive effects," he clarified. "Once a person begins to throw off the heavy energy, his heart becomes more open to the energies of the soul. That makes a tremendous difference, not only to him, but to everyone around him."

I had no idea how much density I might have in my own heart, but I had encountered many people who must have had a lot of it. I thought about a television report I had seen about a wonderful, retired man who was killed on the street. He had volunteered to be a friend to a member of gang, hoping to change that young man's mind about his affiliation. Instead, the boy had robbed and murdered him. Daniel had told me, "When less density meets more density, one of two things will happen. Either the more dense will be transformed, or the less dense will be overcome."

Wide-eyed, I asked another question. "Violence seems to be increasing on the Earth, Daniel. Are there more people with terrible levels of density in their hearts than there used to be?"

"That's one of the tragedies about the Earth," he said mournfully. "Free will allows humanity to set aside its density or accumulate more of it."

Daniel extended his hand and pointed directly in front of us. Within a moment, a shimmering structure appeared. About three times the size of my physical body, a covering like the wings of a dragonfly surrounded it.

"Is that someone's heart?" I whispered.

He nodded his confirmation. Although I knew a heart was meant to turn like a waterwheel, this one hardly moved. The light inside it was coated with the same sticky density that I had battled a few minutes before. Thick, brown energy clogged up the entire structure.

I felt a surge of hope as beautiful streams of silver light poured down over the poor, blocked heart. That glorious energy could only be coming from one source. But it soon became clear that very little of that light was going to find room to get inside the heart. Beginning to cry, I said, "That person's soul still tries to get in! Even though he might abuse other people, or commit crimes, his soul still loves him." I stopped, overwhelmed by the realization that the soul never gives up, no matter what the person does.

Daniel took my hand in his and said softly, "It's the human being who chooses to exclude the soul, never the soul who refuses to come in."

Abruptly, we were surrounded by seven additional hearts. Each was covered with the same shimmering membrane, but some sparkled with beautiful energy, while others seemed to hold varying degrees of density.

I turned my attention to a heart that seemed a little more free. Although density could be seen, it didn't seem to be in every chamber. The heart rotated slowly, but it did move. The light from the soul sometimes found its way inside, and when it did, the particles inside vibrated faster and grew brighter.

Daniel replied to my silent question. "Many people in your country exist in the reality created by a heart encumbered by this amount of density."

"At least some of the energies of the soul can come in," I said hopefully. "That has to make an enormous difference."

"It does," Daniel agreed. "The capacity for physical violence is greatly reduced. But an awareness of the soul is only intermittent and brief. The person accepts externalized standards for his behavior, so he doesn't openly victimize others. However, he's still caught in the belief that everything important exists only in the outside world. He thinks he must overcome others, but he does so in more subtle ways.

"But there are more people waking up to spirit every day. Doesn't that mean they're less encumbered by density?"

He smiled a little. "Yes, it does. They appear strange to the people who have more density in their hearts, because they begin to actually feel the presence of spirit. Intoxicated, they can lose their capacity for discernment and run to and fro with fragments of the truth."

"Parts of the New Age movement." I said weakly. To be sure, the reported encounters with the divine were colorful and often interesting, but they seemed to lack a certain depth. Somehow, I couldn't quite feel comfortable with the crystals hanging from my friend's mirror, or the angel doll placed above her dining table. It seemed every time I visited some of my friends, they were overflowing with excitement about something new.

What had bothered me most about this spiritual dilettantism was that most of the books and workshop leaders never required true, dedicated change. Although they managed to whip up a special kind of enthusiasm, the end result seemed to be a few days of fantastic optimism that was quickly replaced by the same old despair. Then, these people would go on to another source. They repeated their cycle over and over again, always looking for a magical answer that caused no discomfort and provided no real change.

Yet, Daniel had just said people who had eliminated enough density were actually having some contact with the energies of the soul. Perhaps their judgment was a little foggy, but at least they were closer to what really mattered.

"Then there's hope for us!" I exclaimed. "Some people are actually getting somewhere. They're excited about it, Daniel! That has to be good."

"It's very good. But it's important to realize that many people use the subject of spirituality in order to gain more power for themselves. No one can take you home. You have to take responsibility for learning how to do it yourself. Running back and forth from teacher to ashram to workshop will only keep you busy, it won't get you anywhere."

"What happens to the people who get rid of even more of the density in their hearts?"

He stopped me with his answer. "They often get stuck."

"Why?"

"They are able to have enough contact with the soul to keep them satisfied. They often decide to stop their cleaning process and simply bask like a sea lion on a sunny beach."

I smiled as I thought about those deliciously obese mammals lumbering up on shore to soak up the sunshine. They would coo and growl at one another in abject pleasure. When completely satiated, they would roll themselves back into the water and renew their search for food.

Once a person had achieved consistent contact with the soul, it might be tempting to simply enjoy yourself. Eventually, you'd want even more. You'd start to work again—but that could take lifetimes!

Daniel interrupted my ruminations. "Sometimes, what's left of the social mind grabs onto the relationship with the soul. The person becomes consumed with convincing others about the best way to reach spirit."

I had sure known people like that. While they had seemed to be able to tap into a source most of us were unfamiliar with, they weren't always so gracious about their capability. Often, they exuded an air of 'specialness' that seemed ego-driven. These people never seemed to miss an opportunity to proclaim their unusual abilities.

Without so much as an attempt to create a conversational bridge, they would announce, "your aura is particularly bright today," or offer advice about "how to contact your guides." Usually, their audience would react with the expected, "oh my, how do you know that?" which would cause the special one to light up and launch into a protracted soliloquy about spiritual abilities. I had always refused to engage in that particular game and backed away wondering what stroke of whimsy had placed spiritual gifts in the hands of such ribald ego.

But, if I understood Daniel correctly, this was a curious place in the process of spiritual development. Hearts became free enough to receive some of the gifts of the soul. But the social mind was still strong enough to grab a piece of the action for itself. It was similar to the villains in certain movies. Just when the hero thinks his antagonist is dead, he reaches out and grabs his leg. Apparently, a dying social mind would leap into action if it got any chance.

"Many errors are made by those with this level of density who try to offer spiritual advice," Daniel interjected. "If you listen carefully, their messages are filled with strange and mysterious clutter. By snagging your attention with dramatic information, they keep themselves in an important position."

"It's really stuff the social mind is interested in, isn't it?"

He said nothing for a moment and then gently offered, "Very little of such teaching speaks of the need to demolish the social mind."

So many people were desperately looking for spiritual answers. If we let our egos chase after the things that made us feel better, we were going to inhibit our development. "So, even when people are interested in spiritual development, they can end up going in circles."

"You can look at it that way," Daniel replied. "Remember, I'm just describing pitfalls along the way. Every time you cleanse yourself of density, you're doing something tremendously important. Even though each step leads you into another thing to watch for, it's still progress."

"How does density end up getting into our hearts?"

"The social mind breeds anger, hostility, fear, and a desperate need to protect you from others. By holding onto those things in your heart, you clog it up with density."

"How do we get rid of it?"

"Two things are essential," he replied emphatically. "One is to dismantle your social mind and the other is forgiveness."

"Ouch," I blurted. I was thinking about the people with whom I had problems. Some of them had wounded me deeply with their anger or their actions. I had retreated behind a wall designed to protect myself from further pain. But Daniel was saying that I only hurt myself by hiding. Surely, he didn't expect me to get emotionally hit over and over again.

He answered my question before I could ask it. "I'll teach you how you can clean and protect your heart."

"Good!" I exclaimed. "I can see how important it is to keep my heart open, but it still seems dangerous to do that."

He shook his head ruefully. "The dangerous thing is to keep your heart closed! By doing that, humanity is headed toward disaster."

With a wave of his hand, I found myself in the middle of my own heart.

Forty Five

Sparkling light swirled around me in wonderful profusion. I was about to congratulate myself for being so free of density, when an ugly collection of brown and gray energy settled down at my feet.

"How did that get in here?" I asked urgently. I wanted desperately to be able to see and hear my soul all the time. This kind of energy had to be cleaned out!

Daniel appeared in front of me. "Any ideas?" he said innocently.

I hated it when he made me answer my own questions. I didn't want to accept the fact that I had any density, let alone have to acknowledge where it might have come from. Heaving a big sigh, I admitted, "It's probably left over from one of my relationships."

"Why would that be?" he asked maddeningly.

"Because I'm still mad at this person," I said a little bitterly.

"Who does that hurt?"

"Obviously, it hurts me," I replied sharply. Then, feeling a bit ashamed, I added, "This person hurt me pretty badly, Daniel. I'm not so sure I want to go back into a relationship with him."

"Who said that you had to?" he grinned.

"I guess I assumed you were going to tell me that I needed to forgive him, and resume the relationship," I said sheepishly.

"Forgiving someone doesn't mean that you have to subject yourself to more pain," he answered. "It's about letting go of the negative energy you've collected in your own heart as a result of the problems in the relationship."

"How do I do that?"

"Just stop for a moment and concentrate on your heart," he said. "As you do that, think about this person."

I did as I was told, and was surprised to find a hollow, painful feeling right in the middle of my chest. "That's what you've been carrying around," Daniel said quietly. "Now, relax your heart, and allow the love that comes from your soul to flow freely. Don't try to do anything in particular with that spot of density, just let the love come in."

Immediately, the sparkling light became more intense and swirled even faster around me. The density was carried up and began to float.

"Sometimes, it's helpful to pretend that you can see everyone through the eyes of God. Would God have enough patience to love a person lost in his social mind? Would God be able to see beyond his behavior, beyond his words, even beyond all that's negative about him? Would God have enough love to remember the beauty which exists in the person sitting across from you, even when that person's face is contorted with anger?"

I laughed a little and replied, "Obviously, He would. But I'm not God!"

"No, you're not," he agreed with a smile of his own. "But the energy from your soul is very powerful and very beautiful. Now, marshal that energy with your intent. Use it to push that density out of your heart. Give your soul permission to transform the density into something beautiful."

Surprised that I had any control over the energy my soul had given to me, I directed the density out past the boundaries of my heart. It seemed so easy I was astonished. Then I realized that since I had invited this energy in, I had every right to escort it out! What I was doing didn't have anything to do with my former friend. I didn't have to figure out who had been right, or who had been wrong. By forgiving him, I wasn't accepting his behavior or even moving toward resuming my contact with him. I was just taking care of myself. Curiously, as I accomplished my task, my thoughts about him settled down considerably. I relaxed my defenses and found compassion rising where the pain had been. The love that had been buried under my anger began to bloom again, and tears streamed down my face.

"I might want to talk to him again," I choked.

"If you do, that's wonderful," Daniel answered. "But you don't have to. Sometimes, it's even advisable not to resume a relationship. If you forgive someone, it might not change them, but it does change you. If you don't clean your heart, your bitterness and pain only grow. Like a cancerous tumor takes up the room that the healthy organs are meant to occupy, density prevents the full energies of your soul from nourishing you through your lifetime."

"How can I protect my heart and keep it open at the same time?" I asked, still feeling a little frightened.

"By staying in your natural mind as much as possible. Remember, your social mind is the one that counts offenses and feels the pain of being attacked. Your natural mind doesn't rely on others for its energy. It knows the love your soul has for you. If you rest in boundless love, it becomes possible to stay peaceful and safe, no matter what someone else might say or do."

I had to make sure I understood him correctly. "You're not suggesting I just let people run right over me, are you?"

"No," he said soberly. "Because there are so many hearts in the world that are encumbered by density, you need to take care of yourself physically and emotionally. But people end up overprotecting themselves because they're in their social minds most of the time. It's constantly scanning the environment for personal offenses. When you really think about it, much of what you become angry about, most of what hurts you, has to do with feeling threatened. The social mind has no compassion for others and is easily aroused to anger. The natural mind is impossible to offend."

When I stopped to think about it, most of the conflicts I had with people didn't have anything to do with being truly in danger. Sometimes, it was simply their tone of voice, or use of a particular word that set me off. Often, it had to do with feeling unappreciated, or unloved. It was really my social mind that felt offended or scared. On the days that I felt strong, and my self-esteem was high, I didn't respond so quickly to what other people did or didn't do. But, when I didn't feel good about myself, it sometimes seemed the whole world was out to get me. Most of the time, the problem was within me! I was trying to make myself feel better by getting annoyed with those around me. But the answer didn't have much to do with them; it had to do with me shifting over into my natural mind.

Maybe I'd been carrying a misunderstanding about what it meant to be compassionate. I decided to find out. "Daniel, how would you define compassion?"

He smiled. "Compassion is that state in which you have removed all barriers between what you consider 'you,' and 'not you.'

"The barriers made by my social mind, right?"

"Indeed. Every person exists within the heart of God. There is no true separation, except that which is created and maintained by your social minds."

"So, if I enter my natural mind, I can get past the forms and see the divine energy moving within people. Then I can feel compassion?"

"It's more accurate to say that you'll be in a state of compassion," he answered. "When people think they are feeling compassionate, most often what they're really experiencing is pity."

"What's the difference?"

"Pity is feeling sorry for another person from the condition of separation. 'You' are you and the other person is 'not you.'

Although you may extend comfort, it's not true compassion, because you're still on the surface of understanding."

A little embarrassed, I said, "Pity does carry a feeling of 'I'm glad it's not me!'"

Daniel said quietly. "Whatever befalls your companions on the Earth also befalls you. In reality, there's no separation between you."

"So compassion is a loving awareness that everyone exists within the divine flow of energy. We all share the same world. It's kind of like when I hit my thumb with a hammer. My thumb is in pain, but it's not separate from my body. What affects my thumb affects me."

"Very good, Karen!" Daniel said enthusiastically. "Compassion is a difficult thing for many people to understand."

I shrugged ruefully. "But how do I deal with all that pain? I've got enough problems in my own life."

"The pain that's mirrored in others isn't your responsibility to fix. Compassion doesn't require you to solve all the problems of the world. That's the kind of confusion that results in what you call 'codependency.'"

I shook my head. "I'm confused."

"Codependency is a condition of the social mind," he replied. "It's the social mind's way of justifying itself. If you take on everyone's problems and engage in an anxious process of trying to solve those problems, that's the social mind at work. Really, the social mind is just using the topic called 'problems' to get close enough to other people to drain energy from them. When the work of trying to solve the problems becomes greater than the energy your social mind steals from them, anger is the result."

"That makes sense!" I had worked with so many people who were codependent. Although they constantly tried to fix everyone around them, they were also one of the most angry groups of people that I saw. They had a secret agenda: "I'll overextend myself to solve your problems, but I want you to see me as the hero. I want you to admire me and give me what I need emotionally." When that contract wasn't fulfilled by the other person, the codependent would get very angry.

"Compassion calls you to help others in a way that's appropriate. But it also requires you to understand that what others create is theirs to solve. You see, pain, grief, and frustration of every kind are there for an important purpose. They shake you out of complacency. They require that you look beyond the way you have been taught to live. They call you to a place beyond your social mind."

I thought about the times in my life when I had been the most overwhelmed and depressed. Daniel was right. Those times had caused me to see things differently and make fundamental changes in the way I thought and behaved. "So when you're in a state of compassion, it sounds like you simply appreciate the predicament the other person is in and stand as a reminder of spirit."

"Exactly," Daniel replied. "Help when it's right but do it from your natural mind. Watch the ebb and flow of life as it's reflected in the other person. Let the energies of spirit flow through you. Those energies are what the other person truly needs. There's no need to proclaim yourself as a spiritual person. Just allow the light of spirit to shine in your eyes and radiate from your heart. Love and compassion are energies of the soul. Bring those energies into your life and you will begin to receive all the gifts of the soul."

"I'm amazed at all the benefits of moving into my natural mind!" I exclaimed.

He paused for a moment and then asked a surprising question. "Do you know what the purpose of prayer is?"

"To ask God for guidance and strength?" I laughed a little. "I guess people ask God for a lot of others things, too."

Daniel nodded. "The purpose of prayer isn't to offer up a list of what you want God to do for you. It's meant to be an opportunity to center yourself and go into your natural mind. It's very important to take some time each day to focus your attention, and quiet your mind. Remember that you're a child of the divine. Ask to be reconnected to your source. Express gratitude to the one who has made you. Practice the experience of being out of your social mind."

"Nobody ever explained prayer to me like that," I said regretfully. "If people understood what it was really for, we might spend more time doing it!"

Daniel said gently, "Karen, your natural mind exists within your heart. It always perceives the love that's the essence of all things. It knows no judgment; it doesn't label, compare, or compete. It sits in loving acceptance and appreciation for everything and everyone."

I had to say something embarrassing. "It's very hard not to judge. Even if you try to practice acceptance, you still label everything as good or bad, pleasant, or unpleasant, young, or old, etc."

"I know it's hard," he said comfortingly. "Take five or ten minutes in your day and practice seeing your fellow human beings in a different way. Say to yourself, 'for the next few minutes, I'm going to see everyone I encounter as a beautiful creation of spirit. No matter how obnoxious their social minds may be, no matter what they do or how they act, I will see them as containers of the energies of the soul. I will remember that, on the spiritual level, there are only the energies of love going back and forth between us.'"

"That sounds like a difficult thing to do—especially with certain people!"

Daniel smiled. "Look at all the difficult people in your life as spiritual reminders. Each time you struggle with them and feel angry, embittered, and hurt, see it as a reminder that you're in your social mind. In that moment, you've become separated from your soul, for it knows no such feelings."

"Daniel, I finally understand how terrible the social mind really is!"

He surprised me with his quizzical expression. I inquired cautiously, "What's the matter?"

"I think you should see one more thing it can do."

My heart dropped. This feeling had become so familiar. Just when I thought I had everything neatly into place, Daniel would throw something else at me. I couldn't imagine what it might be this time.

The ground opened up beneath me, and I began to fall.

Forty Six

Caught in some kind of vortex, I spiraled rapidly downwards. Like a hapless fly washed down someone's drain, I had no choice but to descend.

"Help!" I screamed to absent ears. No one came to rescue me from my horrifying predicament. "Daniel, help!" Only the rushing sound of turbulent air answered my desperate call.

Like an object spit from a raging tornado, I plummeted without interruption toward the ground. In an amazing free fall, I could see an enormous crowd of people directly below. As I tumbled down to imminent destruction, the cheers of the multitudes roared up to meet me.

The thought that this giant gathering of humanity could possibly be shrieking with delight over my personal catastrophe was at once painful and ridiculous. Obviously, they had no idea I was about to crash like a boulder out of the sky. In fact, their attention was directed toward what appeared to be a man standing before them.

Spinning wildly, flapping my arms to no avail, my heart thumped as fast as my fall. Where was Daniel? There had been no warning that I was about to suffer this horrible death. What could be the purpose behind this impending splat on the surface of the Earth?

My mind coughed up an awful explanation. In this lifetime, I must have jumped out of an airplane without a workable parachute. "All right, Daniel!" I screamed. "I get it! Do I really have to go through this thing?"

Now only a few hundred feet above the ground, I realized I was going to career into the celebrated man at the head of the crowd. Oh my God, whoever he was, his fame was about to end in an ignominious way. What a darkly hilarious report it would make, "An acclaimed speaker was killed today by an unidentified woman who fell without explanation straight out of the sky."

No one looked up to see my rapidly approaching body and, closing my eyes, I braced what was left of me for a terrible impact.

Nothing happened. After a few moments, I cracked open a cautious eye to find myself staring at a huge crowd of expectant strangers, their deep brown skin shining in the intense sun. Where was the man? Was I still alive?

"Dr. Sommerfield, sir?" The man at my side seemed anxious, but not abjectly terrified. Who was Dr. Sommerfield, and where was he?

Looking quickly around, I stood just outside a tattered canopy. The throng before me clearly waited for something. Nudging my arm, the man repeated his question, "Are you all right, sir?"

"All right?" I squeaked. "No, I am not all right at all."

Quickly, he put his strong hand under my upper arm. Another man did the same. A loud voice announced to the crowd, "Dr. Sommerfield must leave now. Perhaps he will be able to return tomorrow." Turning me sideways, the two pulled me away.

Stumbling toward a well-used truck, a jumbled, confusing series of thoughts blew around my mind. What was I doing here? Wait, those people need treatment. Why did I think I knew someone called Karen? No. Don't take me away. I'm not finished with my work. We are making such inroads against the epidemic. We have to keep going. Wait...who is Dr. Sommerfield?

"Let me go!" I urged, pulling away from the men who sought to help me. "Why are we leaving now?"

"You seem unwell, James," a quiet voice sought to calm my distress.

"I don't know what you are talking about," I said, feeling overwhelmingly confused.

"Perhaps the sun," another suggested.

"We have to treat them. There's no one else who can help,"

I stated, struggling to dismantle the spider webs tangled in my mind. "This is no time to be weak."

"You've pushed yourself too hard, James," a tall man spoke softly as he insistently pulled me toward the vehicle. "Night and day, for weeks you've done nothing but work. It's time to rest a bit."

"Rest..." That sounded so good. My knees were conducting their own conversation and falling into the truck seemed like a very pleasant thing to do. But people were dying all around us. We had to keep going! "No, I want to finish with the people who came today. We can't come back tomorrow."

I desperately tried to convey my desire to return to the people who needed me. Gentle hands took advantage of my confusion and directed my tired body into the vehicle. There was so much to be done. Tomorrow, I would be expected in another village. Through blurred eyes, I searched for my schedule. Was it Friday? My muddled brain offered no answer. "What day is it?" I asked wearily.

"It's Tuesday, sir." Seeing the confused look on my face, the aide continued, "Tuesday, October 27."

I pulled the pages of my tattered calendar apart with quavering fingers. My mind caught on the numbers. That's odd. The year 1936 didn't seem correct. I shook off the feeling with a convenient excuse. I must be exhausted.

The battered truck moved through the flat, dusty countryside, jarring its passengers over the prolific potholes in the road. Each bump seemed to free my mind just a bit more, until my thinking became quite clear again.

"Look," I said with renewed confidence. "If we don't get these people inoculated, there's little hope for this region. We'll be able to count the deaths in the thousands."

"You may be right," the man sitting beside me was as dedicated as I was. Sometimes, I forgot to remember that. For three years, Michael had yoked himself to me, working the same hours, and eating the same food. We criss-crossed the country and he stood by my side as hundreds gathered. There was no reason to ever question his resolve.

"You will need salve for that arm," Michael noted. Glancing down, I silently berated myself for allowing my skin to fall victim to the unforgiving sun.

I'm really not suited for this place; I thought with a measure of embarrassment. Now an angry crimson, my usually parchment white skin gave rise to a multitude of red hairs. That hair had been a serious disadvantage when I arrived in this country.

My pale blue eyes were set in a milky white face. The nearly orange shock of hair on my head had caused immediate alarm among the villagers. Half convinced I was some sort of demon; they had scattered in fear whenever I appeared. I had tried to convince them that I had a cure for the awful sickness that was decimating the population. When I brought out my frightening hypodermic, their initial assumptions about me seemed more than validated.

For almost five months, I had pleaded with the village leaders to accept my help. Their own capable healers had cared for them through many different illnesses. But this sickness was unfamiliar. I knew it had been brought here by the Europeans who had invaded their lands without permission.

Making no progress, I had all but given up when Michael appeared. Angular, lean, impossibly handsome, he had approached me one day, just as I had finished making camp. Thinking he was an emissary from one of the leaders I had already made contact with, I tried to communicate with him in an exaggerated pantomime, hoping to bridge the language barrier. After a long five minutes, Michael had spoken in clear, Oxford-born English. Looking at me with amusement, he said simply, "Dr. Sommerfield, I am here to help you." From that day, we had been nearly inseparable; Michael had made it possible for me to treat hundreds of villagers across this beautiful and strange country.

Now that I had been accepted by his people, I had no place among my own. It was unacceptable for a European to treat the native people. They didn't care that a beautiful culture had existed here for thousands of years before they arrived. So many of them hoped the epidemic would rid this land of the 'fearsome natives.' Some even believed this sickness had been sent by God as a punishment for an adherence to native spiritual practices. They cheered at the reports of increasing illness in the distant sections of the country, having the arrogance to assume that same illness would not invade their own serenity.

Somehow, I had escaped from this awful perception of those different from me. I didn't know where I had learned to respect people of all colors, cultures, and religions. Certainly, my own family had tried to instill the false sense of superiority that had fueled so many empires.

From the time I was a small boy, I had been repeatedly punished for asking my father unspeakable questions. "Why would God create people who were inferior to us?"

"He created them to serve us," he had replied, barely looking over his newspaper.

"But father, that does not seem fair to me," I challenged. "Surely, all men and women are meant to serve only God."

"Stop your ceaseless pattering!" he had always retorted. "You were born to govern over the lesser peoples who do not have the intelligence to rule themselves."

My heart had refused to give up, "But father, why wouldn't God give the same intelligence to all the different varieties of people he created? Why would whole groups be born without the necessary ability to reason?"

"Stop!" The dialogue would always end with banishment to my bedroom with the order to contemplate my true station in life.

It always seemed to me that we were all created by God and therefore, we must all be equal. Could God really have sat down one day and decided that whole groups of people would be inherently defective, and in need of someone to tell them how they must live?

My dangerous ruminations had set me up for ridicule at the university. My professors had quoted long passages from various philosophers and tried to argue me out of my strange ideas. Even the church did nothing to support my beliefs. The pastor had used the Bible, and an endless stream of theological reason, to buttress his manifesto.

When I finally decided to become a physician, my parents had hoped my peculiar ideas would finally come to a graceful end. But, after my training, I had quickly decided to serve the disadvantaged. Working incredible hours, I sought to make a difference among the disenfranchised citizens in my city.

After several years, I began to read of the profound need for medical care outside my own country. A space within my heart could only be filled if I answered the call of a thousand voices that rose from afar. I had climbed aboard a steamer one afternoon. Leaving my heritage all but behind, I had sailed into a great adventure.

My new country was filled with a mysterious, exotic mixture of danger and beauty. This glorious land sang her siren's song from the first day I set foot on her shores. I had gazed into countless eyes and found there only profound validation for my curious ideas about human dignity and equality. Though our cultures were certainly different, the light of spirit shined brightly from those eyes in a way so unencumbered and pure. I found myself in the faces of these beautiful people.

My own countrymen had welcomed me at first. But their enthusiasm had shattered in the first attempts at conversation. With the innocence of a child, I had asked questions about their comfortable existence that no one else had ever dared to broach. Their smiles running in fear, each person inevitably excused him or herself. Quickly gathering their superiority along with their wine glasses, they had disappeared into the waiting fold of those whose thoughts mirrored their own.

After a very short while, I was no longer invited to the private realm of the terminally satisfied. It was perfectly all right with me. I had nothing to talk about there.

After Michael had graced my life with his strength, honor, and absolute love, I never had cause to look back to the sterile civility of modern life. I became consumed with work, and there was always more to do.

But I had a terrible secret; one even my beloved Michael knew nothing about. I didn't understand it myself but struggled hard to control my despicable behavior. Inevitably, the desire would rise like a barbarian within me, and I would succumb. Resolving never to do it again, I knew even as I made the promise, I wouldn't be able to keep it. How long would it be before someone found out? How many days would I have until the dark moment when my secret would spring forth in all its ugliness?

I had thought hard about what to do. In the deepest night, I had prayed for relief. Did God ever hear me? It seemed not. In the morning I would be dragged away without pity and forced to repeat my sins.

This power within me was foreign to my precious beliefs and opposed to my nature. Yet, I had to accept responsibility for my actions. Perhaps I did not truly know myself. This poisonous demon had a hiding place within me. His power grew in the darkness. Again and again, he rushed forward to steal my pride and dignity.

It was as though two people carried the name James Sommerfield. One was honorable, trustworthy, and dedicated. The other was ugly, powerful, and relentless. He had only one message: "Do this. Do this. Do this." I could not argue with something that refused to acknowledge my dignity. Throwing myself harder into my work, I fought in silence. But I knew that I would lose.

Again and again, I slid the cold needle into my arm and waited for the delicious sensation to reach my brain. I would surrender to that wonderful place between sleep and wakefulness, only vaguely aware of my surroundings.

My health was declining. I knew it most painfully on days like this. Hundreds of villagers had lined up to see me. They celebrated my existence and welcomed me with gifts and boundless love. Never had I been so treasured. Today, I had been unable to fulfill my promise to those people. I had betrayed their trust. Because of me, they wouldn't receive their inoculations against the sickness that blew through their country like a terrible wind. If some died, it would be my responsibility.

How did I arrive in such a despicable place? Always, I had sensed the devilish force inside. As a small child, I knew of the split within me. As though living two lives, I built my existence around the effort to contain the darkness dwelling deep in my heart. Terrible self-condemnation tore apart my ability to find internal peace. I lived in torment, adding numbers to my armies of honor only to watch them crumple in defeat when my powerful foe decided to appear.

We had journeyed for several hours toward the village which lay to the north. Making camp, our tents glowed from within like the fireflies that scattered over the darkness. The night stretched out its welcome, bringing with it a thousand creatures of beauty. The frogs and crickets sang their praise to the universe and wishing my friends a restful sleep; I went into the embrace of solitude.

Pacing back and forth, I struggled once again with the shadows eclipsing my soul, "Do this. Do this. Do this." Finally, my will bent like a crumpled piece of paper, I accepted the command of the barbarian. Tears of defeat strewn across my face, I quietly punctured my skin with that long, slow movement I both hated and adored.

This time, even as I drifted off, I knew I would never awaken.

Forty Seven

My wail of grief careened off the barren hills that surrounded me. Through deep sobs, I heard Daniel's voice beside me. "It's all right, Karen. It's all right."

I opened my eyes. "But, Daniel," I whimpered. "It's so sad. James' life was so tragic."

"Indeed," he answered, a clear note of melancholy in his simple reply.

"But, why?" I gulped. "He was such an extraordinary man. Whatever that was inside him destroyed his life.

Taking a brief look around us, I had no clue about where we might be. My mind sent up its patter of concerns, but I shook them off, and asked, "Was that really me?

"It was," he answered. "You met an early death."

I asked the foremost question in my mind. "I didn't mean to kill myself, did I?"

"Of course not," he replied. "You had a lot of work you wanted to accomplish on the Earth."

"Then, what happened?" I cried. "Why did I die that way?"

Looking over at me for a long moment, Daniel finally said, "Elemental grew and grew until it enslaved you. Eventually, you lost all judgment."

I braced myself for the imminent arrival of what would probably be another mind-blowing fact about life on Earth. What else had I never known about before meeting Daniel?

To me, the word elemental only meant that something was basic. What had overtaken poor James? My next question was as brief as my understanding. "Elemental?"

"A particular vibrational energy field exists around the Earth," he began. "Its purpose is to activate the physical senses so that the lifetime on Earth can be perceived through the body. Elemental is a special kind of density that has solidified in parts of that field."

Maybe I hadn't understood him correctly. "Are you telling me our ability to use our capacities to taste, touch, hear, smell, and see comes from spiritual energy and not just the structures of the body?"

"Of course," he nodded. "You see, those abilities are activated to different degrees in people so that they can gather particular information needed by their souls."

"That's certainly a different way to understand how our senses work. Wait a minute," I added excitedly. "Our psychologists have only recently discovered the fact that each person has a favorite way to take information in from the environment, and process that information."

"Yes," Daniel replied, amusement clear in his voice.

In territory I thought I knew something about, I rushed forward, "Some people seem to be inherently visual. They see pictures in their minds very easily. Their language indicates that ability. They describe their world in terms of images and use phrases like, 'I see what you mean,' and 'let's look at another way of looking at this.'"

"Go on," Daniel said, now openly beginning to chuckle.

"Well, others are kinesthetic. Their way of thinking is reflected in the body. They simply 'get a feeling' about something or know it without seeing pictures in their mind. They use phrases like, 'I can grasp what you are saying,' and 'that idea knocks me over.'"

"Yes," he prompted, doing an excellent approximation of an eager graduate school student.

"And then there are the auditory people. They hear a running dialogue in their own mind. Sometimes, it gets so loud; they don't hear anyone else very well. But it's just their way of dealing with reality. Their thinking gets turned into commentary."

"And their language?" Daniel said with a smile.

"Well, let's see," I stopped to laugh at my how my choice of words indicated my own perceptual preference. "Here's a good one, 'I hear what you're saying,' or 'that rings a bell for me.'"

"And," he asked wryly, "Do your psychologists have an explanation for why these differences occur?"

"Hmm..." I paused, trying to remember my text books. "I guess they just believe a person is born one way or another. But it doesn't come from genetic material, does it, Daniel?"

"No. It comes from the intention of the soul that is activated by the energy field around the Earth."

"Wow." I allowed the new information to sink in. "Depending on which sensing ability is the most activated, the person will notice different things in the world. He'll be aware of certain parts of reality, while someone with another sensory emphasis will be aware of other things."

Clearly humoring me, Daniel asked, "Do your psychologists say this?"

"Well, yes they do," I nodded.

"All an intent of the soul," he said quietly, lifting his sparkling eyes to watch a puffy white cloud drift by.

"Something must have gone wrong with this system along the way! You said that elemental was a special kind of density that had solidified around Earth. Did the vibrational field get clogged up somehow?"

"It still exists and functions," he replied. "But now, it is dotted with slow-moving and thick energy."

"Why?" I exclaimed.

"Free will," he said patiently. "As the social mind grew through the ignorance and choices of human beings, the senses became subordinate to it. The sensory capacities aren't used to discover what the soul wanted the person to learn. Instead, the senses became misdirected instruments of an unabashed quest for stimulation."

"So, the social mind just got hold of the senses and decided to have itself one wale of a good time," I said disgustedly. "It took the instruments that were to be used for the soul's purposes, and abused the privilege?" Humanity seemed to have taken advantage of every opportunity to shoot itself in the foot when it came to spiritual progress.

"Yes," Daniel said softly, gracefully extending the back of his hand to a wondrous blue butterfly. It accepted the invitation and vibrated with contentment.

Shaking my head, I tried to make sense out of the information I was being given. "Daniel, I've got a piece missing here. How did density end up in the vibrational field and what does that have to do with elemental?"

With a sad sigh, Daniel said, "The willingness to release the capacity to see, smell, touch, taste, and hear is noticeably absent in many human beings at the point immediately after their death."

"Go on."

"Even when the social mind decides to allow reabsorption into highest self..."

"And not become an entity," I interrupted.

"Yes, and not become an entity, the activated senses can be left behind. Remember, these senses are forms of energy." Daniel advised. "One must be careful not to think of them as eyes, ears, mouths or skin."

"Okay." Taking a big breath, I continued, "The parts of the energy that allowed a person to perceive through his senses, can get left behind after death?"

He nodded.

"And that's free will!" I exclaimed. "Those capacities don't have to be reabsorbed into the highest self if they don't want to?"

With a little smile, he emphasized my statement, "They can't be if they don't want to."

"Are you saying that there's a collection of other people's activated sensing abilities floating around in the energy field that surrounds the Earth?"

"Yes," he replied, and watched me squirm with this very uncomfortable information. Seeing that I was ready for more, Daniel went on. "Sometimes, a being coming into a lifetime hits one of those dense collections around the Earth. That misfortune can have terrible consequences."

"Daniel, are you saying that a person who passes through one of those dense spots around the Earth ends up with hyperactive senses?"

"Yes."

A light went on in my head. "Alcoholism, drug addiction, sexual addiction. Are those difficulties the result of elemental?"

"Often, elemental is a powerful contributor to those painful problems."

"Oh my God." The last forty years had seen a wonderful shift from the view that addiction was a moral defect, to medical and family dynamics perspectives. Many believed that addiction was genetically determined. Others had decided that dysfunctional families created such pain; individuals were trying to self-medicate to relieve it. Meanwhile, the most effective treatment options were still centered around twelve-step fellowships.

Daniel was saying that addiction was truly a spiritual problem. It had its genesis in our entry into the Earth plane. But surely everyone still had to take responsibility for themselves. I shrugged and said, "What can people do about this? They can't just excuse themselves with a statement about elemental. 'Well, you know, I flew through some bad energy in my journey to Earth. I think I'll just indulge myself.'"

"Elemental can be starved to near extinction. Every time a person chooses to perform the problem behaviors, elemental grows stronger. Eventually, it will overtake and destroy him. But, if elemental isn't fed, it will weaken and fade away."

Something finally made sense to me. "That's why an alcoholic can't just have one drink, and a drug addict can't have a hit just one more time." Amazed, I exclaimed, "No wonder James felt like he had a demon inside! Elemental was pure, raw sensory need. It didn't have a thing to do with who he truly was."

"Elemental grabbed him repeatedly. Eventually his heart was burdened with self-hatred and fear."

I felt grief rising in my chest. "Once he felt so bad about himself, he lost the ability to receive much from his soul, didn't he?"

"Sadly, even when the heart was originally free and clean, a spiritual bankruptcy occurs as a result of giving in to elemental. The person can no longer hear the voice of his soul or feel its energies. Even if the soul is able to break through, the person doesn't feel worthy of its love. He turns away from the thing that can solve everything."

Pausing for a moment, he added, "If elemental has been allowed to grow and grow, there's only one thing to do."

"What is it?"

"He must work incessantly to destroy the capsule of the social mind. Only by encountering the energies of his soul can true liberation from elemental be found."

"But that's so hard to do when you don't know you're stuck in that capsule!"

"The predicament for most of humanity," he agreed.

"That's why organizations like Alcoholics Anonymous have been successful. AA's first step is to admit that you have a terrible problem."

Daniel nodded his agreement. "The social mind is dedicated to protecting itself. The last thing it wants is to be exposed. If the person can show himself or herself to others as he is and not as what he wants others to believe that he is, that's a wonderful beginning."

"James was so secretive. He needed help, but he wasn't willing to ask," I said sadly. "He wasn't able to speak about his struggle to his closest friend in the world."

"The social mind doesn't want its mask to slip," Daniel said quietly. "Humility, vulnerability, and a willingness to admit the need for help are not qualities of the social mind."

Tears filled my eyes, "So, James' own social mind conspired with elemental to kill him."

"I would think it would be of help to addicted people if they knew that they were caught in the sensory refuse of those who died. It would certainly increase my motivation to free myself."

Daniel continued, "Each person can rise up, and refuse to allow the foreign energy to ruin his life. If he can understand who he truly is and accept the unending love from his soul, he will have the energy with which to overcome his opponent.

"Day by day, sometimes hour by hour, the person must decide to live his life as the embodiment of refuse, or as a reflection of his soul. By tuning his awareness he can come to recognize which energies are his and which are not. He can learn to identify and conquer elemental before it overwhelms him."

I thought about an oil spill I had helped to clean up when I was in college. A black, sticky goo had covered the beaches in Santa Barbara. Thousands of sea birds lay helpless on the oily sand. Their wings were so burdened by the foreign substance; they could only flop around helplessly. I had wept over the pitiful creatures. They were so separated from their inherent abilities. It seemed those encumbered by elemental were in the same predicament. But no one knew about their invisible enemy.

Welcoming me back from my ruminations, Daniel continued, "To win over elemental, the person must never allow himself to spend time with those who are busy feeding their own elemental energy. Proximity to that kind of energy only causes his own to rise eagerly to the surface."

Something else occurred to me, "Daniel, he was so debilitated by elemental and so cut off from the voice of his soul. Wouldn't that leave him horribly vulnerable to entities?"

It seemed such a person would be like a sick animal lying on the ground, just waiting for something stronger to come along and finish him off. Weak, confused, and discouraged, he would be eaten alive!

"A person who is in the grip of elemental is terribly vulnerable to entities," Daniel answered.

"I bet some entities had their own addictions when they were in their own bodies. If they invade somebody who is actively using alcohol or drugs, they can continue to experience that addiction."

"Exactly."

I continued. "That would make the living person's addiction much, much worse, wouldn't it?"

"Yes, it would," he confirmed. He got up and began to walk up the side of one of the hills.

"Where are you going?" I called after him.

"Come along!" he answered. "It's almost time."

"Time for what?" I said, scrambling to catch up with him.

"You'll see," he answered mysteriously. "You'll see."

Forty Eight

We walked over the top of the hill, and I could see that a crowd had gathered below us. They talked excitedly with one another. Clearly, they were waiting for something.

"Where are we?" I asked Daniel. While I was grateful that he hadn't sent me to this new location alone, I was shocked to see that we seemed to be in a different time and culture.

There were only two women among us, but men with deep brown skin stood together in small groups. They were dressed in simple clothing. Rough in texture, it seemed to be made of cotton and flax. Looking down at myself, I wasn't surprised to see that I was covered in a long, yellowed garment. My hands told me that I was again occupying a male body—a body that seemed to have spent long hours working hard in the hot sun.

Since Daniel had not answered my initial question, I decided to try another one. "What are they waiting for?"

"Their teacher," he replied cryptically, and craned his neck to see over the crowd. "He's an excellent one. Well worth listening to."

It was warm here and there was no breeze. Surrounded by low hills, we lingered in a small valley. A few men struggled to light torches. Others began to gather brush and placed it on the side of one of the hills. Soon, they had managed to build a small fire. Clearly, they hoped the teacher would stand near the source of light so that all could see him.

Suddenly, the crowd buzzed with excitement. Then, they grew absolutely silent as a tall man came into view. He walked alone, his bearing regal and filled with strength. But he was not a braggart. He exuded a wondrous sense of serenity and compassion.

Climbing up on the hill, he stood exactly as the crowd had hoped he would—right in front of the fire.

Dressed in a long, white garment, he wore a simple brown rope around his waist. Long, dark hair was swept back and gathered with a leather string. As he looked over the gathering of people, I saw that his skin was as black as midnight. But startling clear blue eyes illuminated his interesting face. He was a long way from being handsome, but it did not matter. He radiated the kind of beauty that came from deep inside. Extending one hand, he motioned for the crowd to sit down. Without hesitation, we sank to the hard ground, almost in unison.

Anticipation rebounded off the hillside as we waited for him to speak. No one dared to breathe, afraid that even that simple action might cause us to miss a single one of his words. The man closed his eyes for a moment and then sent a beautiful baritone voice out over the crowd.

"Hello, good people."

My mind faltered, and my heart nearly leaped out of my chest when the crowd answered:

"Hello, Jesus."

Forty Nine

Spellbound, my eyes were locked on the man's face. How could this be Jesus? Could Daniel really have given me the opportunity to hear Jesus speak? My mind flopped wildly, like a fish leaping in and out of the water. I was dangerously close to passing out.

He spoke with aching compassion, "In an ecstatic dance, you are held within the embrace of boundless love and forever cherished. In the silence between each of your breaths, your soul whispers its encouragement and guidance. It waits for you to return to your awareness of its presence. If you are willing to grow beyond the confines of what you have been taught, you will hear your soul sing to you. Only you can decide whether to continue your imprisonment or fly into freedom and again know all the love of whole."

The man before us began to glow with an awesome light. It radiated from his face and hands, soon obscuring the fire behind him. That light fell over the crowd, touching our hearts and igniting the love which had been dormant within us. All around me, people had started to cry, their faces filled with joy.

He continued, "There is no Lord and Master. Do not try to make me so. Do not follow me and never worship me. I am not your king. I cannot save you from yourselves. Go instead toward your own soul, for that is your true lover. Go into the arms of love, and not into the prisons of confusion, and loneliness. Never be afraid to know your own soul. It holds no judgment. It offers only limitless love.

"Open your heart, for that is the only way home. That which you guard so carefully, will often be wounded in this world. But if someone hurts you, do not close your heart and hide. Do not seek to wound him in equal measure. Instead, turn your other cheek toward him and offer it to be wounded as well. Know that this action provides you with another opportunity to cast away the hardened energy which surrounds your being. Say to the others, 'Go ahead, tear off my false face. Wound everything I think that I am. Wound everything I think I should be. Strip away everything, but my heart. For my heart is the only thing that is truly me.'"

His voice rose with passion, and he said, "No one can give you the experience of God. I will light the path for you so that you may find your way. But you must open your own heart, for this I cannot do for you. Your religious leaders do not teach you how to go to the center of your heart and therefore, they are only distractions. The way you become perfect and beautiful is not by following rules and standing before your priests. Instead, throw open the doors of the prison in which you hide. Throw open your heart and call to your soul. Ask that it take your life, broken and confused as it is, into its arms. Know that it is there that you belong. Ask that your soul clean you, soothe you, and love you. Know that if you are not in the arms of the soul, you will never be perfect and beautiful, for it is only the soul that makes you so."

Suddenly, the crowd gasped with awe as three luminous figures appeared very near the teacher. Made of magnificent white light, absolute devotion and joy radiated through them. They joined hands and then, made a circle around him. Smiling broadly, he spoke again. "It has been said that three men came from the East shortly after my birth. Indeed, there were three who came to be with me on the Earth. But they were not men of flesh and bone, but spirits sent forth by my soul. These spirits make up my being as they do yours. They do not literally come from the East, but from the realm of illumination, for which you have made the East a symbol. Cherish these spirits which are you. They each bear instructions from your soul."

The teacher extended one hand, and the crowd cried out as he held out a beautiful, spinning sphere of incredible gold and platinum light. "I have also heard you say that a special star guided these men to me. Know that the star of Bethlehem was a planet, much like the Earth. On that planet lived many people who had started their spiritual journey long before you did. They progressed so rapidly that, at my birth, their world and all its inhabitants burst with the light of heaven and returned all the way home. This magnificent display ushered in a new time for the Earth—a time in which you will have special opportunities to learn and grow. If you use what you are taught, the Earth can be like its sister planet and explode in glory. You can take yourselves home."

Throwing the sphere high above him, the man smiled. The ball of light traveled at an amazing speed, straight up into the night sky. There, it burst and brilliant sparks fell down over the assembled people. The bits of light landed directly in our hearts, sending an ecstatic wave of love through our bodies.

Now, his words came softly and gently, "Dedicate yourselves to spiritual development. As I have taught you, do not become entangled in the hopeless prison of your mind, but think instead with your heart. From this place, you can greet your brothers and sisters, and you will need nothing and offer everything. In this way, peace will come to the Earth. Remember, you cannot serve two masters. You must decide whether you will use your lifetime to further the wishes of your soul or give it to your social mind.

"There is a guiding plan for the Earth's people. If you open yourselves, and seek to reunite with your souls, you can receive all the benefits of the divine plan. You never walk alone but are always accompanied by spirit. Take the help that is offered to you, put yourselves under the direction of our plan. In this way, you will always know why you are on the Earth, and what you need to do in order to grow."

"These things I tell you so that you may make your way toward your true home. Take what you have seen and tell others. I ask that you spread this news among all the people living in your world. But be sure that you tell them that I cannot bring anyone into the heart of God. Each human being must do his or her own work."

"But know, with every breath, with every beat of your heart, in every moment of your life; know that you are deeply and constantly loved. So it will be forever."

As quickly as he had come, Jesus was gone.

Fifty

We sat together for a long time; no one wanted to break the magic. Gradually, people began to climb to their feet and talk to one another. I waited until Daniel stood up and then followed him.

"Watch what happens," he said quietly. He moved amongst the throng, stopping to listen for a while and going forward again. Finally, we stepped beside a cluster of four men and one woman.

One person was speaking in a low, almost conspiratorial tone. A giant of a man, his arms were thick with muscle. Long, cinnamon-colored hair sprung from his head in a disorganized flurry. "We'd better figure out how we're going to translate Jesus' message to ordinary people."

"Translate?" The woman's head was covered with a soft blue hood. She was young, perhaps only 20 years old.

"Well," the man sounded slightly annoyed. "We certainly can't go to our neighbors and tell them exactly what we have seen. They will think we're demented or possessed by demons. And the priests will come after us. You know as well as I do, what our teacher said is directly contrary to what they have told us we must do."

"I think we should take that chance," the woman answered courageously. "It is only by telling the truth that we have any hope of affecting anyone. What he said and showed us was so beautiful, so filled with love, so compelling, can anyone turn away?"

"Women," the man scoffed to his friends. Smiling and nodding at him, they began to move away from the woman. Clearly a peaceful person, she allowed them to leave her and went quietly into the darkness.

"The first thing we have to do is organize," another man said. "If we take his teaching and put it into a form that everyone can accept and understand, we'll have a much better chance of being heard."

A nervous man with intense brown eyes spoke. "I know how to write."

"What use is that?" the big man laughed. "No one knows how to read."

"I think it's important," his friend answered. "I want to be sure that his teaching is preserved."

"Do what you must. But, for God's sake, don't say anything about that ball of light or the three spirits. We saw those things, but other people won't be able to see them. You know how people are, if they can't see it or hear it, they don't believe it exists. Besides, if the priests get hold of that, we'll be stoned to death. What good will that do anyone?"

"What about the information he gave us about our souls?"

"Why don't you just use the word God? People already worship God. It's much easier for them to understand. Just write that they must work hard to be better people. Then, they can be with God."

"Stop it!" I shouted, unable to take their intent to distort the spectacular teaching I had just witnessed.

"They can't hear or see you," Daniel whispered. "I want you to watch what's happening."

"But it's terrible, Daniel," I cried. "This is how Jesus' teaching got all mixed up in the first place. You're the one who showed me what terrible consequences that has had for humanity. Can't we change things right now?"

"That would be a violation," he replied, only inciting my anger.

"Daniel," I said through clenched teeth. "I'm sick to death of free will. All people do is use their freedom to make a mess of things."

"Nonetheless," he began.

"I know, I know, Earth must always be a place of free will." My stomach was tight, and my heart pounded with contained emotion. It had taken so little time for the teaching to be distorted. Like a wagon with one wheel off track, humanity was going to go in circles for two thousand years because of the lack of courage of these men. Bitterness surged in my throat as I thought about the millions of people who would die in the name of this wondrous teacher.

The big man continued, "It's important that people know who to follow. The only way they'll do that is if they believe that Jesus will truly change their lives. They've been waiting so long for a king to arrive. They need someone to respect, someone who can save them from their hardships."

"Jesus said we were not to consider him a king," the nervous man said.

"Well," the larger man mused. "I know he did. But he also charged us with the task of getting his message across to ordinary people. You know how he is, sometimes I think he doesn't under-stand that the people who come to listen to him are special—we're really not like the others. It's our job to be the bridge between Jesus and the rest of the people. If they don't follow him, how are they going to learn from him? I don't think he would object to that. How else can we get things done?"

"You do have a point," the others nodded in agreement.

"Daniel," I said desperately. "Please, can't we do something?"

"That would be a viol-"

"Never mind," I interrupted. I didn't want to hear that again. I was beginning to fully understand how frustrated our souls must be with our inability to use free will to help ourselves.

"Spirit is not given to frustration," Daniel said quietly. "We will wait for humanity forever. It is you who suffer."

"Arrgh," I muttered, stomping my foot on the ground.

"Nobody even knows that Jesus was black! The picture I had in my Sunday school showed him with blond hair!"

"People knew that until about the fourth century," he replied calmly. "Then, the leaders of the Christian movement decided that Jesus should be portrayed as a more comfortable figure to the people they wanted to convince. At the same time, they hid all of his teaching about reincarnation in the belief that people would be more motivated to follow his teaching if they thought they only had one life on the Earth."

Letting the issue of reincarnation go, I asked, "Were there many black people in Israel?"

"Only a few," he answered. "Jesus chose to live within a body that had black skin in order to stand out. It was easier for people to accept that someone entirely different from them had this startling new information. You see that in your world today."

He was right. After trying to share my first series of adventures with Daniel, I could easily see that people expected such information from exotic places, not from somebody just like them.

I decided to ask something about which I had always been curious. "Daniel, why are there different races of people on the Earth?"

He smiled gently. "Can't you figure that out?"

"Well, I think it's delightful to have diversity. It would be pretty boring if we all looked the same. But that can't be the reason."

"In a way it is, Karen. The lessons of the Earth are all about opening the heart and allowing the love of spirit to flow through you, and out into the world. When you are confronted with diversity, you are exposed to a wonderful test of your capacity to apply what you came to the Earth to learn."

"So, are you saying that the different races gives us opportunities to strengthen our capacity to open the heart?"

"It's like the weights I've seen you lift to build your muscles. If you always used the same weight, you'd never grow stronger.

By increasing the stress, you gain new ability. At this stage of their development, most human beings pull their energy in when they're in the presence of differences."

"Are you saying there will always be a certain amount of tension between different groups of people?"

"Only until you all learn to open your hearts and keep them that way. Until then, each meeting with someone of a different race, gender, religion, sexual orientation, or culture, is a test of how much you've grown, and how willing you are to keep trying.

"We have a long way to go," I said sadly.

"When a person is uncomfortable, he or she must learn to recognize that the social mind is clamoring for control. Racism has many terrible roots that lay tangled under the surface of the mind. As you seek to destroy those roots, they multiply and send up ugly new growth. The social mind is an expert at nurturing what's directly opposed to spirit. By doing this, not only are those whom you regard as different from you greatly harmed, but the social mind gains control over the hearts and minds of those who do the rejecting. Such ugliness in one's heart contaminates the energies of love. The soul can't find its way into such a heart, and the person destroys himself in the process of trying to harm others."

The men turned and walked away into the night. Daniel said quietly, "As you have just seen, the birth of Jesus marked the beginning of a wonderful opportunity for Earth's people to learn about who they really are. But his message was horribly distorted, and the extraordinary opportunity was missed. Now it's time for humanity to have a second chance."

"What about the divine plan Jesus talked about? I've never heard of such a plan."

"Karen, that plan has been confused beyond description." Daniel looked at me for a long time and then took my hand. "If humanity can understand it again, the terrible predictions about

Earth's fate need never come to pass."

My heart began to pound, as I waited for him to explain. Instead, he catapulted me into a completely different environment.

Fifty One

I stood on an enormous platform of sparkling amber light. Like a giant record, it rotated clockwise and seemed almost flat. A few paces away from me, a large, mysterious hole compelled me forward. Gathering my courage, I stepped to its edge, peered over, and gasped. Off in the distance, I could see the Earth. Exquisitely beautiful, the glorious blue planet was surrounded by empty space.

Mesmerized by the sight, I didn't dare to move. Sensing Daniel behind me, I cried, "Where are we? The Earth looks so small from here!"

"You wanted me to tell you about the plan for the Earth," he said matter-of-factly. "I couldn't explain it unless we came here."

"But where are we, Daniel?" I turned around and found him calmly watching me.

"Remember, I've told you that the Earth is a kind of school?"

"Of course I do. Earth is a place where we can regain our spiritual awareness."

"Well, a school has to provide classes for its students. Otherwise, no one can learn."

"Yes," I replied. Daniel's expression told me that he thought I should be able to put the pieces together and understand what he was trying to tell me. But I still didn't have a clue.

He patiently waited for me to say something but finally gave up. "Karen, this place provides the curriculum for the Earth's people."

"Huh?"

Grinning, he seemed to enjoy my confusion. "Each year, there are twelve different classes for the people of Earth. There are many levels of understanding that can be gained in those classes. It's impossible to learn everything by going through only once. That's why you rotate through them many times."

I shook my head in a futile attempt to clear away the mental cobwebs. Looking out across the plane of light, I couldn't understand what it had to do with providing lessons for the Earth. But I was suddenly sure of one thing. He had said that there were twelve classes each year. "Daniel, is that why we have twelve months in our year?"

"No," he said bluntly. "The months and their names are an artificial construct placed over the natural environment. But it's interesting that twelve remained an important number, even though people had no idea why."

"Well, tell me how it works!" I exclaimed.

Daniel extended his hands to draw my attention back to the plane of light. "Karen, what does this place appear to be made of?"

"Energy." I was glad to have an answer for a change.

"Indeed," he smiled. "It's made of twelve different kinds of energy."

"Okay," I said tentatively.

"The Earth is exposed to each of the twelve different kinds of energy in succession. The energy that covers the Earth at any given time helps to bring you to a new level of understanding about some very specific things."

"Are you saying we're literally showered with our lessons?"

"You could say that" he agreed. "The energy bodies of human beings have been constructed with the same kinds of energy that exist in this place. When a particular type of energy flows over the Earth, it makes its corresponding energy vibrate more quickly. When that happens, your awareness of a particular part of your true nature is increased."

I looked at him with amazement and said, "But the lessons rise up from within us. They're stimulated by different energies from the outside, but they only remind us about what's deep inside, right?"

Daniel replied. "All the answers come from within you. That's why it's so important to pay attention to the intuitive wisdom that speaks from within your heart."

"Has this been going on for a long time?" I had never heard anyone talk about anything like this. Could it be that we were all being stimulated by special forms of energy, but we were so dense, we couldn't feel them?

"We've given you this opportunity since the beginning of your time on the Earth," Daniel replied, sounding wistful. "But, like so many things, you've ignored our help and twisted this information into something that's no longer correct."

I stared at him for a moment and then said, "These twelve types of energy come in succession, but they're not connected with the months of the year. How do we know what kind of energy is being directed toward us? How can we know when it changes?"

Daniel grinned and then knocked me over with his answer. "By looking at the zodiac."

"People have always assigned spirit to the sky. Of course, spirit exists everywhere. Heaven isn't above you, and neither is your soul. When humanity forgot about the true origins of the spiritual energy directed toward Earth, it still searched the sky for answers."

♥

Fifty Two

"Good Lord, the zodiac!" I gasped. "You aren't telling me that astrology is true, are you?" Like many people, I couldn't help but read my horoscope online each day. However, I had never really believed that the planets directed the course of my life. Astrology had seemed so simplistic, even fatalistic to me. I believed strongly in self-determination. The idea that my fate had been sealed by the location of certain celestial bodies at the time of my birth was depressing.

"Relax, Karen," Daniel laughed. "Astrology is a distortion of the original teaching about the twelve types of energy. It was developed in Babylonia in the first millennium BC. The Egyptians added more confusion, and the Greeks contributed the mathematical computations that you use today."

"Is there anything in astrology that's correct?"

He shrugged. "Amazingly, there is. Like most of the spiritual teaching on the Earth, terrible distortions are mixed together with fragments of the original information. Intuitively, people know that astrology contains something that's important for them to understand. Otherwise, interest in it would never have survived for all these centuries."

I hadn't thought about astrology that way. Maybe the compulsive need to read my horoscope wasn't that odd, after all. Perhaps many of us couldn't ignore the information because we felt it was strangely applicable to our lives. We just didn't know why.

I straightened up, as though adopting a stronger physical posture would help me to assimilate what he had to say next. "What's accurate, and what isn't, Daniel?"

"Well, there are twelve signs in the zodiac, and twelve types of energy. But that energy has nothing to do with the movement of the planets. It comes from spirit. But oddly enough, the order of the energy is reflected in progression of the signs."

"What about the dates for each sign?"

"Still correct," he nodded. "The dates for the shifts in signs are the dates for the shift from one kind of energy to the next."

"What about the symbols for the signs?"

"Pure fantasy," he replied. "People have always assigned spirit to the sky. Of course, spirit exists everywhere. Heaven isn't above you, and neither is your soul. When humanity forgot about the true origins of the spiritual energy directed toward Earth, it still searched the sky for answers. The stars were viewed through a process of psychological projection. They became animals and gods that were then associated with the different signs in the zodiac."

I liked his answer. Born under the sign of Pisces, I hadn't particularly enjoyed being represented by a pair of fish. "What about the characteristics that are associated with each sign?"

"Well," Daniel began, "what is now thought to be characteristics of the signs are what are left of the original teaching about the twelve kinds of energy. You're all exposed to these energies, and so, you could say that each of you contains all the signs."

"So, it really doesn't matter when we were born?"

"Not in the way astrology would have you believe. However, the type of energy being directed toward the Earth at the time of your birth is important. The lessons stimulated by the particular energy present at your entrance into the Earth plane, will be of special importance to your growth."

"Is that an accident? Does the soul choose which type of energy it wants its creation to be most exposed to?"

"Often," Daniel replied. "Of course, with the advent of your specialized medical procedures, births do not always occur at the time the soul would like. Many couples fear that they are infertile. In fact, the soul of their baby is simply waiting to create a body so that it will be born under the desired energy. Since a particular energy only occurs once a year, it can take a lot of time for them to become pregnant. There is nothing physically wrong with them, at all."

"Wow," I uttered, instantly thinking of the friends I had who were anxious about not getting pregnant right away. Some of them had even gone through dozens of tests, only to be told that no cause could be found for their apparent infertility.

Daniel continued, "Once the zodiac was developed, people began to believe that the only information that was relevant for them was that given for their own astrological sign. This is tragic because it separates people from one another. By accenting the differences between signs, human beings continue to fall into the hands of the social mind. This division of 'you,' versus 'them,' is false and harmful."

Excitement rushed through me. "But you're saying that we're all exposed to the same sequence of energies each year! It's like going through high school. Nobody sits in one classroom all day long. Every hour or so, everyone shifts to a different teacher and learns different things."

"Indeed," Daniel answered soberly. "As I have told you many times, you weren't sent to the Earth to be alone, confused, and afraid. By providing you with these energies, we're trying to help you to remember who you really are. If people know about the help that's available, they can band together. They can be on the same page of their lesson book, so to speak."

"You know," I said sadly. "About the only time we do anything like that is during the Christmas season. Despite the commercialism, there's still a certain magic in the air. There's an energy of optimism and goodwill. We seem to have more trust in one another. And it's depressing when the holiday's over. We all go our separate ways, back to our own lives and our own concerns."

"Exactly," he replied. "Although, I have to say that Christmas falls on the wrong date."

"It does?" I squeaked and geared myself up for another surprise.

"If you truly want to celebrate the date of Jesus' entrance into the Earthtime, you need to move Christmas to March 6."

My head began to hurt—a lot. Not only did Jesus look radically different than I had been taught he did, but his birthday was celebrated on the wrong day. Somehow, the idea of Christmas in March wasn't very appealing.

Even though my mind begged me not to do so, I ventured a question. "If his birthday is in March, how in the world did it end up in December?"

"Winter solstice," Daniel said quizzically. "The beautiful celebration about Earth's rhythms became confused with Jesus' birth. It's lovely symbolism. The darkest day of the year is followed by increasing light. Jesus came to help humanity rise out of the darkness and regain its rightful place in the realm of spiritual light." He paused and grinned. "Also, the stories about his birth have to do with the particular energy being directed to the Earth at that time. But I'll explain about that later. It's not really important which day Christmas is celebrated. I just thought you might like to know."

I stared at him for a moment, not knowing whether to be angry or grateful. My mind violently objected to having the pieces of my reality tossed about like pickup sticks. But my heart was enlivened and eager to hear more. I would never turn away from what Daniel had to teach me. I just wished the process could be more comfortable.

Taking a big breath, I asked, "Are you going to tell me about the twelve energies?" I knew he would say yes. The question was just my way of telling him to proceed without having to take responsibility for whatever happened next.

"Of course," he replied brightly. Taking my hand, he pulled me forward across the plate of light.

"Let's begin."

Fifty Three

As I gazed across my new location, I had a compelling sense that I had been here before. Luminous currents of blue, green, and purple swirled past me. I looked around, strangely certain I would see my soul.

"Very good, Karen," Daniel said appreciatively. "That didn't take you very long, at all!"

"What?"

"The first type of energy is sent to the Earth during the time you have called Pisces," he replied. "I'll use the familiar astrological terms for each of the energies. That way, you won't get so confused."

"The zodiac begins with Aries," I protested. Quickly stopping myself, I didn't need to hear his answer. Clearly, that was something else that had gotten mixed up.

"The energies of Pisces are meant to stimulate your memories of being united with your soul. You're encouraged to disengage from the aspects of your life that come from your social mind and focus on the attributes of spirit. You remember that everything is part of one living mosaic of love. This energy helps you to recover your natural abilities—intuition, creativity, extrasensory perception, and communication without words."

I stared at him in amazement. "Everybody on the Earth receives this energy? We all have a chance to recover those abilities?"

He smiled over at me. "Remember, these are inherent capacities of all human beings. Because you are mesmerized by science and worship the brain, you're amazed when another person demonstrates the abilities that you've forgotten you have."

I thought for a moment. "I bet we can't make much use of the energy if we stay inside our social minds."

"No," he said sadly. "If you needed water but refused to go to the place where it could be provided, you would never receive it."

My heart was pounding with excitement. "Daniel, if we go into our natural minds and accept this shower of energy, what will happen?"

"With several experiences in this energy, some people develop the capacity to step outside of their familiar mind-body self and can see spiritual reality. Deep compassion and wisdom are the result. Over time, a wonderful sense of the magic in your world returns. Everything and everyone you see becomes beautiful. An intense desire to help animals and other people rises within you."

"I was born under this kind of energy, Daniel. I'm amazed at how it's affected my life!"

He smiled and began to walk away. "Perhaps you can see why Jesus chose to enter his body at this time."

"Wait a minute!" I called after him. "If the two fish aren't an appropriate symbol for the first energy, then what is?"

I could hear him chuckling up ahead of me. "A star, Karen. Think of the first energy as being represented by a star."

I was about to ask him to explain why a star would be the appropriate symbol. But I remembered that we could see the stars as pinpoints of light in the top of our social mind capsules. That light came from our soul and called us to break free.

"Tell me about Aries," I said, following him into a distinctly different kind of energy. Red and orange, it moved rapidly around my legs and carried a mildly uncomfortable electrical charge.

"This is the energy of the newly born personality," Daniel replied. "Filled with optimism and drive, it reminds people that they have been given the opportunity to have a lifetime on the Earth so that they can work hard for their souls. Their commitment must be to their souls, not to the demands of the social mind. It stimulates them to overcome all obstacles that might get in their way. It inspires courage, honesty, and dedication to their purpose, and reminds them that their time on Earth is too short to waste."

"So, it's really a time to renew our commitment to our souls. We need to remember to take our lives in the direction that was meant for us and not get lost in the demands of our social minds."

Daniel looked pleased with me and continued. "This energy provokes uncompromised idealism, a desire to right the wrongs the social mind has done in the world. But it also provides a reminder to return to innocence—everything that is done in the name of the soul must be motivated by an uncomplicated desire to serve."

As I stood in the midst of the energy, a curious series of feelings went through me. I became impatient, and an unfamiliar nervousness demanded that we move forward. I had books to write and people to talk to. There were so many things I had to do if I was going to get Daniel's message out into the world.

He grinned at me, and said, "Good. You've experienced what this energy is designed to stimulate. You can think of the second energy as being represented by an eagle. This beautiful bird lands on the Earth but uses its strength to soar toward the heavens."

Eager to obey my urgent desire to get going, I walked away from Daniel, and hoped he wouldn't allow me to get lost. Soon, I had crossed a border and was embraced by another type of energy.

Vibrating quickly, this energy sang a wonderful, rhythmic melody. Deep green, cinnamon, and cobalt blue, it was sensuous, luscious, and warm. "We must be in Taurus," I said, finding my body slowing into a delicious sense of comfort.

"I'll remind you that I'm only using the astrological names so that you don't get confused," he answered. "This is the third type of energy being directed toward the Earth."

"Hmmm," I murmured, and settled into the lovely sensations that rose from the energy.

"When we give you this kind of energy, we're reminding you of Gaia and the Creator. We're stimulating you to enjoy the natural beauty around you—to see the colors, to listen to the birds, care for the animals, and keep the oceans and the rivers clean. You're nourished spiritually and physically out of the generosity of these two beings from heaven. If you will tune yourself to their rhythms, you can have first hand experiences with the beings who came from the same place from which humanity fell long ago. Gaia is your mother, your sister, your lover, and your companion through all the days of your life. The Creator offers the masculine energy that provides balance, and a different kind of strength. He gives you all the animals that serve as your examples. Bless these lovers. Care for them. Remember what they have given."

By the time Daniel stopped speaking, I was crying. Like so many people, I was often so caught up in my own concerns; I forgot that the Earth was incredibly beautiful. "What's the symbol for the third energy?" I asked through my tears.

"An ancient sequoia tree," he replied. "Although it stays grounded in the earth, it continually reaches high toward heaven."

He gently took my arm and pulled me to my feet. Wiping the tears from my face, he said softly, "There's still time for humanity to save itself. Hopefully hearts will awaken, and people will remember who they truly are."

Fifty Four

We made our way to the fourth kind of energy—something we had mistakenly called Gemini. Remarkably different from that of Taurus, it didn't flow or offer any comfort. Instead, tiny balls of shiny silver and platinum light bounced erratically all around me. "What's going on here?" I asked, feeling distinctly uncomfortable.

Daniel chuckled and said, "The fourth energy stimulates the understanding that there's no true permanence to anything except the soul. Everything can change and usually does. It's unwise to try to create absolute certainty and stability. You are meant to shift between the various aspects of your being. It's best if you can flow easily from the realm of spirit into your life on Earth, and back again. This energy reminds you that you're not simply a personality, but also a larger consciousness that temporarily resides in the body. With time, you can learn to swim freely between the self that you have on the Earth, and the Self that's much greater than that.

"Why does this place make me feel so uneasy, Daniel?"

"You're standing in the field of creativity and change," he answered. "Remember, all things appear to have solid form, but they're really only temporarily invested with energy. Most people have subscribed to the idea that what they see is permanent. When it shifts, you want to find a way to nail it down and stop the movement. This makes for a lot of anxiety. You're not permanent; physically, emotionally, or intellectually. If you let go of the concept of permanence, you gain the ability to move with the flow of energy and no longer set yourself against change. You become able to act in accordance with the tides of energy, and the result is creativity, joy, and an increased awareness of the constant movement of life and spirit. It's like the difference between observing a photograph versus participating in the events that will be solidified in the photograph."

"Or like trying to freeze the flow of a river versus jumping into the river, and floating where it takes you?"

"Exactly," he replied. The symbol for this energy is the cloud. One moment, it can be powerful and compelling, sending rain and even lightning to the Earth. Then, it disappears, only to emerge again." Daniel walked away from me, clearly ready to show me the fifth energy.

Filled with a transparent, shimmering silver light, the next energy was rotating slowly. I knew we had entered the time that astrologers called Cancer. A deep, resonant pulsing sound seemed to rise beneath my feet. As I paid attention to it, the sound became distinctly familiar and rhythmic. "That's a heartbeat!" I exclaimed, looking at Daniel for an explanation.

"Indeed," he answered. The fifth energy reminds you that the true center of your being isn't the mind, but the heart. It's in your heart that you can hear the voice of your soul. By changing your awareness of yourself so that you become heart-centered, you begin to leave your social mind behind.

"The energy stimulates your awareness that all human beings contain the light of their souls. Your task is to remember to look for that light, no matter how unattractive their social minds may be at any given time. Sharing from your heart liberates you from the isolation, secrecy and shame that are the by-products of the social mind. It invites you to constantly take risks, to uncloak yourself, to seek intimacy, and drop the shell of protection that prevents you from giving and receiving love. If you offer love from the deepest part of your heart, you cannot be harmed by anyone. This kind of love comes from your soul and does not need anything in return. Its source can never dry up. By opening yourself, you become more alive, and more able to receive from your soul. But it's essential that you cleanse your heart frequently. Otherwise, it becomes clogged with emotions that don't belong there. You become a passive victim, riding on endless tides of fear, anger, resentment, and depression that are born of the social mind."

He steadfastly walked away, and I scrambled to catch up with him. "What's the symbol for the fifth energy?"

"The heart, of course."

"Liberate yourself from the old beliefs that you do not deserve wonderful things. Accept all that is given to you. Use this energy to break free and release yourself from inhibitions. Reach out to everyone around you. Offer the love that swells in your heart. Leap into new experiences, and know that no matter where you go, or what you do, your soul always surrounds and loves you."

♥

Fifty Five

Instantly, I was thrilled to be in the sixth energy. A brilliant, sunny yellow, everything around us seemed to radiate joy. A childlike silliness bubbled up within me, and I wanted to run and play in the exuberant light. "Daniel, this place is wonderful! We're in Leo, right?"

"That is the mistaken name," he answered. "Enjoy the energy, Karen. It is meant to stimulate happiness. By integrating your body, mind, and heart, you can overflow with happiness. The Earth surrounds you with love and abundance. Your soul showers you with love and countless blessings. When you bring yourself into alignment with who you really are, you free yourself to enjoy all the bounty of heaven and Earth. You are alive! You have been given the opportunity to learn, grow, and expand beyond every limitation. There is no reason to stay inside your fears. Stand up and allow yourself to love. Stretch beyond the boundaries your social mind has imposed and receive all the gifts that surround you. Liberate yourself from the old beliefs that you do not deserve wonderful things. Accept all that is given to you. Use this energy to break free and release yourself from inhibitions. Reach out to everyone around you. Offer the love that swells in your heart. Leap into new experiences, and know that no matter where you go, or what you do, your soul always surrounds and loves you."

I was giggling uncontrollably as I scooped up the beautiful energy and threw it high into the air. Millions of tiny, yellow fragments of light drifted down over me, and increased my self-confidence and joy. I felt I could do anything.

"Whee!" I yelled into the air. "Daniel, it's amazing to me that we haven't known about this energy. It's so powerful; it seems we wouldn't be able to prevent ourselves from responding."

Daniel looked serious for a moment. "You must be careful to do the work of dismantling your social mind. Otherwise, it can misinterpret the energy, and egotism can be the result. You want to experience the love and joy that come from the soul, not sensory overindulgence, and distorted self-confidence that come from the mind. When you stay connected with your soul, you never forget that all good things come through you and are not of you. That way, these energies don't cause you to swell with arrogance and pride but stimulate you to remember that spirit is the cause of everything. Other people are never seen as less than you, or not as important as you are. Everyone sparkles with beauty and abilities when their hearts are open to the energies of their souls. Joy is the greatest teacher of all."

"And the symbol?"

"A field of flowers," he replied. "Spirit nourishes you, just as the sun allows the flowers to open and reveal their beauty."

I knew before he said it, that it was time to leave this wonderful place. Like a small child who doesn't want to leave the playground, I planted my feet and briefly entertained the idea of refusing to go. Then, I remembered that this energy would rain down over me and everyone else on the Earth, during a very special time of the year. When that happened again, I would be ready! Like a happy puppy, I followed after Daniel and found myself in a very different place.

An icy, pale blue, the seventh energy seemed very serious. We had to be in Virgo. The exuberance I had experienced slowed, and I became calm and still inside.

"Look closely at this energy," Daniel said quietly.

I bent my head and peered cautiously into the space right around my feet. Now, I could see that the energy was comprised of lovely small rods of light. It wasn't all one color, as it had initially appeared to be, but was filled with hundreds of subtly different shades of blue. Amazed, I glanced over at Daniel. "I had no idea there were so many blues," I exclaimed.

"That's the purpose of this energy," he answered. "It reminds you to focus your awareness, and to become proficient in discerning one type of energy from another. Without that ability, you're left to perceive in a clumsy manner. You miss the details, and can blunder in your interactions with spirit, the world, and other people. This energy stimulates your ability to notice the small things, and to treasure the times when your attention is totally in the moment. It calls you to sharpen your awareness of the energy bodies that make up your being, and to be sure they're cared for. It draws you toward time alone—time in which you can steady yourself and remember who you are. The energy reminds you about your purpose on the Earth and asks you to bring your focus to doing what your soul wishes you to do. It's the opposite kind of energy from that of the sixth place. But opposites are really only two sides of the same thing. A life without time for quiet contemplation is a life that's quickly lost to the demands of the world."

My breathing had slowed, and my body had relaxed. I was thoroughly enjoying watching the energy. Now, I could see the movement of light within each rod, and the variations of blue continued to amaze me. I realized how much I lumped things together in ordinary life. Blue was blue—the category contained thousands of shades, but I was too busy to be aware of them. I noticed the trees, but how often did I stop to examine a tiny flower? A loud noise never failed to command my attention, but did I listen to the sound of the wind in the trees?

"Very good, Karen," Daniel whispered. "Just as an artist paints with both tiny strokes and larger ones, so your awareness must be used to its full capacity. The symbol for the seventh energy is the weaver. An intimate awareness of thread, each color and texture is necessary to compose a beautiful tapestry. Then, he smiled and said at full volume, "Let's go! Time to experience the eighth energy."

I followed him straight into Libra.

Radiant and beautiful, she opened her arms, and I went straight into them. There, I could feel the love of my soul being transmitted through the heart of my natural mind. A wonderful sense of peace permeated my being. I looked up into her luminous face and saw the reflection of heaven in her eyes. She sparkled with joy and endless compassion, and I nestled against her, content to stay there forever.

Fifty Six

"I think I already know what this energy is about!" Standing in glorious pink and silver light, I could see my natural mind up ahead of us.

"Hello, Karen," she said. Radiant and beautiful, she opened her arms, and I went straight into them. There, I could feel the love of my soul being transmitted through the heart of my natural mind. A wonderful sense of peace permeated my being. I looked up into her luminous face and saw the reflection of heaven in her eyes. She sparkled with joy and endless compassion, and I nestled against her, content to stay there forever.

"You send the eighth energy over the Earth to remind us of our natural mind," I said. There was really no need to formulate a question. I already knew there could be no other reason.

"That's right," Daniel replied. "Because humanity has developed the social mind, it's necessary to help you remember your natural mind. Unfortunately, most people have no idea that the social mind is an enemy in their midst. It rules over their lives, causes misery, and prevents them from sharing in the abundance of spirit. During this shower of energy, many of you shift rapidly from the familiarity of the social mind into the natural mind, and back again. This can cause an uncomfortable fluctuation in emotions, personality, and behavior. Until humanity remembers the true nature of its being, and chooses to stay in the natural mind, it will experience a certain loss of equilibrium under the influence of this energy. Rather like being caught in an earthquake, a person may desperately attempt to find his balance, only to find that it's futile. The energy is more powerful than his desire to find an unmoving place within himself."

"But when we know about our natural minds, then this energy must feel absolutely wonderful!" I cried. "I've experienced what it's like to slip out of the clutches of my social mind. Once I'm in my natural mind, everything becomes beautiful and peaceful. I can see energy moving all around me. I can feel how deeply my soul loves me."

"It's very sad to watch what happens when you get lost in your social mind," my natural mind said softly. "I can't do anything to help you. Karen, you are such a sweet, gracious, and loving person when you are with me. But, when your social mind grabs you, you become anxious, depressed, and confused."

"I know what you mean," I sighed. "I also know that I waste a lot of time trying to figure things out intellectually. Meanwhile, all I really have to do is shift over to you, and everything becomes absolutely clear."

As my natural mind held me close, she said, "Much of the time, you desperately try to find harmony within yourself. But that isn't possible inside the realm of your social mind. It struggles to eliminate everything that is wonderful about you. Your intellect becomes impaired, your creativity is interrupted, and your loving heart becomes clogged with anxiety."

Daniel added, "You're not the only one, Karen. Most people are engaged in the same struggle. We send this energy to everyone, so that each of you can feel the pull of your natural mind and make a concerted effort to find it again."

My natural mind backed a few feet away from me, and whispered, "Remember, I am always with you. I am who you are meant to be while on the Earth. My symbol is the waterfall. It represents the endless supply of energy and love that the soul wishes to pour into every human being."

Love shined from her eyes, and my heart swelled with gratitude. Then, Daniel took my hand, and we went on to the ninth energy.

Fifty Seven

Shocked at what I was seeing, I turned to Daniel for an explanation. Red, orange, and purple energy boiled around us. Intermittently, jagged silver streaks crackled by, and provoked feelings that I didn't want to have.

"Don't look from the perspective of your social mind," Daniel advised quietly. "Of the twelve types of energy, the one you know as Scorpio is the most misunderstood and misused."

He was right. Surprised by the forceful energy, I had shifted out of my natural mind without even realizing it. Now, I tried to detach from my environment and closed my eyes. Using what Sally and the others had taught me, I focused on my heart, and took several, very deep breaths. When I opened my eyes again, everything was different.

The energy was much calmer, and now moved in beautiful circles, like the eddies in a quiet river. The silver streaks had become integrated with the other energy, and now pulsed inside the orange and red, like the light of fireflies on a hot summer night.

"My goodness, what is this place all about?" I asked.

"Passion," Daniel replied.

"What?" Surely, he wasn't talking about sexual energy. Humanity didn't seem to be lacking in that.

"This energy is sent to the Earth to spark an intense desire within each person."

"An intense desire for what?"

"Many people are very complacent about their purpose for being on the Earth. They have little passion about their bodies, their minds, or their souls. They drift along, always meaning to do something purposeful tomorrow, or next month, or next year. Somehow, they never quite build enough desire to break free of their old patterns. They stop growing and devote their lives to an endless series of responsibilities. Their bodies become slow, and their minds are filled with anxiety and depression."

I interrupted, "And they forget about their souls."

"Indeed. But you see, the social mind has become so powerful, unless a person can find a true passion to liberate himself, it stays in control. Daniel paused for a moment and then added, "There has been much consideration about not sending this energy to the Earth."

I was surprised by his statement. It seemed to me that we needed much more passion, not less of it. "Why would you even think about not sending it?"

He shook his head sadly. "When a person is firmly caught within his social mind, the energy is misused. He becomes filled with passion, but he misdirects it. Rather than ferociously insisting his way out of the social mind, the person becomes a warrior for its causes. He's seized with anger at other people. He righteously defends his boundaries from the imaginary injustices done to him by others. The social mind grows bloated with power and pulls the person into a series of wars with the people around him. Or it beats him down, until he isolates himself, and wallows in self-pity and depression."

"I can see what a difficult decision this must be for spirit," I said sympathetically. "If we don't find enough passion to fight the social mind, we won't get anywhere. But, if social mind grabs that passion, and uses it to build more power for itself, we go backward. I would think a person could spend a lifetime chasing imaginary demons and never open his heart."

"So it is," Daniel replied. "This energy provides a wonderful opportunity for people to become invigorated again. They can increase their commitment to escaping from their social minds.

They can feel the excitement of the lover who waits for them and rededicate their lives to their spiritual growth."

"This energy can be like a massive jump-start for everyone on the Earth!" I cried.

"Or, it can be a terrible stimulation of the social mind," Daniel said quietly. "Fire is the symbol for this energy. It can be terribly destructive, or it can serve to ignite that which is absolutely necessary for human survival." He murmured to himself, "At some point, we will have to decide whether to continue to send it."

I was ready to leave this place. I didn't need anyone to help me bring up the passion needed to dismantle my social mind. Although it was cunning and powerful, I knew I didn't want to live inside its dark realm. I renewed my decision to stay with my natural mind and walked in the direction that Daniel now pointed.

Catching up to me, he pulled me past what seemed to be a very light-hearted and playful field of energy. Wait," I exclaimed. "That looks wonderful! Why aren't we stopping?"

Daniel smiled broadly and said, "This energy is so important, I want to show it to you after you've had a chance to experience the eleventh and twelfth. Don't worry. We'll come back."

Reluctantly, I followed him into what had commonly been known as Capricorn. "This is an odd place, Daniel," I blurted. Unlike any of the other places we had been, this energy was azure in color and seemed almost still. It seemed stable and strong, but I was puzzled about its lack of movement.

"Passion must be united with steadfast determination," he answered. "Otherwise, you'll never find your way home."

I thought for a moment and then appreciated what he had said. I knew plenty of people who talked enthusiastically about spirit but didn't seem to get any closer to their souls. Instead, they seemed to run after new teachers, took lots of classes, and came up with new plans to further their growth. By the time I talked to them again, they were already onto a different idea.

"Finding your soul isn't complicated," Daniel said. "But it requires patience and clear, unwavering commitment to do what must be done."

I nodded, "If I don't do what Jessie, Sally, and the others taught me, it won't help me. It's up to me to take the time to apply what I've learned. If I don't constantly confront my social mind, it will take over completely. I have to remember why I'm here on the Earth. I have to act to further my growth. Nobody is going to come along and do my work for me."

"Exactly," Daniel replied. "It's not enough to think casually about spirit. It's not enough to challenge your social mind once in a while. It's not enough to take the time to find your natural mind every so often. If you give up when times are hard, you'll miss the best opportunities to apply what you have been taught. Only with dedicated, passionate desire will you make your way home."

I looked at him for a moment and then smiled a little. "I completely understand why this energy is so necessary. What is the symbol for it?"

"The waves of the sea," he replied. "They never stop. They never doubt their destiny. Their steady power can break apart the largest obstacle and change it into tiny grains of sand. With determination, you can transform your social mind and release its energy back into the whole."

He paused a moment and then said, "The twelfth energy supplies humanity with some of its most difficult lessons. Come, I'll show you."

Fifty Eight

I swallowed hard as we entered into the realm of Aquarius. Millions of tiny dots of brilliant white light were suspended in darkness. As I watched, they moved toward one another and began to form intricate patterns. Like the whirring of a humming-bird's wings, a gentle sound accompanied their progress. "What's going on here, Daniel?" I whispered; afraid I might somehow interrupt the beautiful designs that were emerging all around us.

"Just watch, Karen," he replied quietly.

Now the dots moved into the shape of a thousand luminous hands. Reaching toward one another, the hands joined and formed giant circles, as though hundreds of people were connected with each other. Suddenly, I could hear singing. At first, it was barely discernible, but the volume steadily increased until an enormous choir of men, women and children thrilled me with spectacular, multi-leveled harmony. The words seemed to be in many different languages, but the sound was full of hope and joy.

Barely daring to breathe, I looked over at Daniel. His face was filled with the same brilliant light as he swayed back and forth in rhythm with the song. I let myself go, and soon my body answered the music. A wonderful sense of belonging to something much greater than myself brought a deep sense of peacefulness into my heart.

Suddenly, I understood the words they were singing: "I honor the light in you...and also in you. We are all making our way to the same place. I honor your journey...and also yours. We all come from the same source. Together, we will find our way home...home to purest love. That is what we are made from...that is what we are. Together, we will find our way home."

Tears streamed down my face, and I didn't need to question Daniel about what the twelfth energy was for. Humanity needed to be reminded that we were all in this together. There were truly no differences between us, except those made by our social minds. We all had the same work to do; we all had the same destiny. If we remembered that, we could help each other. We weren't meant to be isolated and alone in our quest. Only by supporting and encouraging one another could we find what we were looking for. The knowledge that we were all striving for the same thing could be our common ground. No matter what cultures we came from, no matter what languages we spoke, our journey was the same. We all wanted to find the love we remembered deep in our hearts. We all wanted to go home.

"That's right, Karen," Daniel said softly. "The symbol for this energy is the human hand. Reaching out for one another is essential, but it often seems terribly difficult. Take the risk. When you hold back, you go in the opposite direction from your source. Learn to love in every situation, no matter how hard it may be. Open your heart and allow others to know who you are. When you have no secrets, then you will find joy."

I closed my eyes and let myself go. Like a kite in a gentle breeze, the song seemed to carry me higher and higher. I heard Daniel say, "Go ahead. Glide on the energies of love. That's how you'll find your soul."

Ecstatic, I soared on the music until I landed with a thump on cool, damp grass.

Fifty Nine

Although it was dark, it seemed safe to assume I was back on the Earth. As usual, I had no idea why Daniel had taken me to this particular place. "Daniel!" I called into the night. "I thought we were going to go back to the tenth energy. Why am I here on the Earth?"

Receiving no answer, I unscrambled my legs, slowly stood up, and scanned the environment for a clue about where I might be. Off in the distance, I saw the lights of a small city. Ruefully, I mulled over the fact that I could be anywhere from Boise to Katmandu.

"There's still time, you know." A tiny, lyrical voice wafted out of the darkness.

"Hello?" I called tentatively. By now, I knew to brace myself for the unexpected. Who knew what Daniel might be up to this time?

A small girl emerged from the night. About seven years old, I could just barely see her face. She seemed oddly familiar.

"What are you doing out here?" I asked gently, trying not to frighten her. "It's late. You should be home with your parents."

"Came to see you," she answered simply. Her striped shirt sent bright colors into the darkness.

What was it about her? I struggled to see her face, but I was sure I had seen this child somewhere before. "Do you know where we are?" I asked lamely. I was the adult here. I should be the one to know where we were.

"Yep," she said comfortably. Her bright blond hair was bound in a cheerful ponytail.

"Well," I prompted. "Where are we?"

"Santa Barbara," she said proudly. "I know my street, too."

Santa Barbara! Again, I called silently for Daniel. What in the world was I doing in Santa Barbara? I had grown up in this coastal town in California, but I had left years ago. Why was I here now?

"Well, let's get you home!" I said to the little girl.

"No," she answered with the kind of finality that usually announces a tantrum in the supermarket.

"Look, we have got to get you back where you belong." I scrambled to come up with a plausible explanation for whomever we might encounter. Let's see, "I was walking down the street in Boise, Idaho, and well, I went through some of my lifetimes, spent spectacular time with my soul and now I'm here. This girl appeared and well...here you are...no need to thank me." I don't think so. Maybe, I could just walk her up close to her front door and hide in the bushes somewhere to make sure she was all right.

"You always try to get me to stay where I belong. But I belong with you," she said strangely.

"But," I sputtered, "You don't even know me. How could you belong with me?"

"Just do," she replied, plopping down a few feet from me.

What was it about this girl? I still couldn't see her face clearly, but she was so familiar.

A certainty about who she was popped into my head. "Daniel! It's you, isn't it?"

To my complete surprise, I heard her begin to cry. "What's the matter?" I said gently. I had no desire to upset her, but I also didn't want someone to find me here with a child in obvious distress.

"You never remember me," she gulped.

How could I know this child? We lived hundreds of miles apart. "I'm really sorry," I said, frantically looking for a way to make her feel better. "Sometimes, I get so busy, I don't notice little kids the way I should."

"That hurts my feelings," the girl said sadly.

"I'm really sorry," I offered soothingly.

I thought about all the times I had said a quick "hi," to children without ever really paying any attention to them. They lingered in the background while I went on with my conversations with adults. I sometimes treated them like a piece of furniture. Inevitably, they would eventually find a way to interrupt us. Always feeling aggravated, I did nothing but hope their parents would quiet them somehow so we could continue. But how would I feel if a visitor came and went without really acknowledging my existence? It was not surprising they often became dramatic in their attempts to be recognized.

Searching for something to say, I gazed toward the city a half mile or so away. It looked different somehow—there were fewer lights than I remembered.

"I want you to play with me sometimes," the girl suddenly announced.

"I'm sorry. I can't play with you. I don't live in Santa Barbara."

"That doesn't matter. You just don't want to," she replied, her small voice quivering. "I've given you a whole bunch of chances."

Afraid that she was about to break into full-blown sobs, I struggled to distract her. "What kinds of things do you like to do?"

In amazement, she replied, "You don't know?"

"No," I replied a bit defensively. Then softening, I tried to calm her, "I'm sorry, but I really don't know."

After an accusing silence she said quietly, "You would if you ever talked to me."

Feeling annoyed and compassionate at the same time, I was getting very worried about my predicament. This clearly wasn't the place to sort out my relationship with a kid I didn't even know.

"Look, we have to get you home," I said using a tone parents often resorted to when trying to control a child. Standing up, I struggled to think of a way to placate her. "Look, maybe sometime I can come visit you."

"That's what you always say," she responded, obviously not ready to let it go.

"I do?" She must have me mixed up with another adult.

"Yep, you do," she confirmed. Then, she sighed and continued, "But, you get busy, and then I don't get to talk to you for years and years."

"Years and years!" I protested. "For heaven's sake, you're only about seven years old."

"Years and years," she emphasized. Taking a big breath, she continued, "And, I have lots of things to tell you about...like how I want to play, and how some of the things you do scare me, and how I get tired of waiting around, and how I don't like some of the big people you have to see, and how..."

"Wait a minute!" I interrupted. "How could you possibly know what I do and who I see?"

"Cause I'm with you all the time," she answered, hurt still caught between her words.

This little girl was very strange. Wanting to end the conversation and get on with my own concerns, I decided to try again to find out who she was, and how to return her to her home.

"What's your name?" I said very calmly. "Please tell me your name."

"I'm Kari," she said solemnly. "I'm Kari Alexander."

Sixty

Alarmingly, I was actually starting to get used to this feeling of being hit between the eyes with a metaphorical two by four. Ever since I first met Daniel, events had continued to conspire with the obvious intent to shatter my mind.

I leaned toward her and finally managed to see her small face. Indeed, it was the same one which had stared back at me in countless black and white photographs I had seldom taken the time to look at. "You're me?" I managed to squeak.

"Yep," the girl replied, watching me struggle to put myself back together.

I sat down beside her and surveyed the familiar gray-blue eyes. Wait a second, the city lights I had searched for...maybe they weren't there. "Kari," I said, using the calm, slow voice people usually reserve for mental patients, "What year is this?"

"Um," she pondered. "Um...um...1959." Then wanting praise for her answer, she asked brightly, "Is that right?"

Shaking my head in an effort to settle my brain, I replied, "You know, I think you are right."

"Oh that's good," she said happily. "You don't think I'm right very often."

"Kari...you know what?" I said sadly.

"What?"

"I didn't even know you were there." Of course I had heard about the concept of the inner child. Numerous books had been written on the subject. I had incorporated those ideas into my counseling practice, but she wasn't a theoretical construct. She was alive!

"That's what makes me sad," Kari said, her voice trembling.

"I knew you were there as an idea, but I didn't know you were as real as you are." That suddenly sounded like a very stupid thing to say.

Obviously agreeing, Kari pronounced, "That's dumb!"

"Yes, it is dumb." I had no reason to argue with her. She was so beautiful, so clearly bright, and alive. She was me before all the nonsense of my life got in the way. Daniel had taught me that I was an energy system, not just flesh and bone inevitably tied to linear time. Now 38, I acted as though all my previous years had disappeared behind me. But maybe people were really more like trees. Each year of our lives was still contained within us, just like the rings in a tree.

"Do you see everything that goes on in my life?" I queried.

"Most of it, except when I decide to hide. Then, I don't see anything except the other me's."

"The other you's?"

"Yep," she answered. Suddenly, another child appeared before my eyes. In shock, I temporarily forgot how to form words and stared in silence.

"She's nine," Kari said. She introduced her matter-of-factly, like a child bringing a friend to meet her parents.

"Hi," the new child said confidently.

Shakily, I said, "I guess I'm surprised to see two of you." That was another stupid thing to say, I thought instantly. My energy system was plenty big enough to sustain several inner children. A tree didn't just have one ring, and now it was clear that I didn't just have one inner child.

"There are lots of us!" Suddenly, the seven-year-old looked pleadingly at the nine-year-old, and cried, "I think we should tell her some things before we go."

"Go?" I said lamely. Where in the world did they want to take me? I wasn't prepared to romp around Santa Barbara with two small children in the middle of the night.

Before I could ask, the seven-year-old said, "You don't pay any attention to us, and it makes us sad. Besides, we have lots of ideas for how to fix things."

"Fix things?"

"Yep," she asserted. "Like when you get scared about something, it's usually one of us who's really afraid. If you'd just stop a second and talk to us, then you wouldn't have to be scared either."

"I guess I do have to do a lot of things a kid wouldn't like very much." I said apologetically. "And I don't know how to talk to you."

Both girls giggled. "You just do it. You just stop what you're doing for a minute, and tell us you'll take care of us, no matter what."

"That would really help you?" I asked.

"Yep," they answered. "Sometimes we forget that you're there. We start thinking that we have to do whatever you're trying to do. We're too little to take care of certain things. So, we get really scared. If you don't remind us that you're big enough to face things, we get even more scared. Sometimes, you end up getting scared because we are!"

"That makes sense," I said softly. I thought about the odd anxiety that sometimes crept up from deep within me. The funny thing about it was, often I hadn't been able to put my finger on what was making me anxious. I had shaken it off and told myself I was being ridiculous. But, if one of these children inside was really who was frightened, my method had been very cruel.

"And," the seven-year-old chimed in, "when you start getting tired and mixed up, I think we should just all stop and play."

"I bet you have good ideas about how to do that," I said.

"Yep. But you usually tell me they're stupid," the child replied sadly.

I considered all the times I had wanted to take the day off to fly a kite, see a silly movie, or just lay in the grass, and find pictures in the clouds. She was right. I always told myself I was being lazy and then threw myself harder at my work.

"I'm very sorry." I said regretfully. "That must not feel very good at all."

"No," she answered flatly. Issuing a huge sigh, she added, "We just hope for another day."

"And," the nine-year-old contributed, "some of the people you hang around with...well, we don't like them very much."

Maybe that little voice of warning that rose up within me sometimes belonged to one of these kids. So often, I had tried to like someone, only to have my initial negative impression confirmed.

She sat down at her feet and fidgeted with her shoelaces. Clearly, there was something else she wanted to say. "It's all right," I said reassuringly. "Go ahead. Tell me."

"Well," she whispered. "Sometimes, I just want to sit down. You're always running around so fast. I get tired."

She was right. I didn't stop and allow myself to do nothing very often. Somewhere along the way, I had decided that I should be constantly productive. If I wasn't seeing clients, I had a class to teach. When that was over, I would launch a new project. My mind was in a continual whirl, always planning things to do.

"And another thing," the seven-year-old said quietly. "We don't know how to do everything. And we know you don't know how, either. We get really scared when we don't know, and you don't know. But you go and try to do it anyway."

That really hit home. I had a habit of getting in over my head. Then, I would frantically try to figure things out as I went along. On countless nights, I had stared at the ceiling of my bedroom, and worried. Habitually, I agreed to do things without thinking them through. I liked my adventurous spirit, but did I really need to create continual anxiety for myself?

If these little girls really lived within me and experienced everything that I did, I was going to have to find a way to take care of them. By doing that, it seemed I would be relieved of much of my unexplained anxiety and fatigue. Besides, they could bring a lot of happiness back into my life. Maybe I could rediscover the joy and exuberance that had been missing for such a long time.

I asked, "Back there, you said that there was still time. What did you mean by that?"

"Still time to meet the most special one," she said reverently.

Puzzled, I offered, "Even though I haven't always acted like it, I think you're very special. But you want me to see somebody else?"

"Yes!" the two yelled simultaneously.

"She talks to us sometimes," the seven-year-old announced proudly.

Before I had a chance to answer, she shouted, "There she is!" Eyes wide, she looked over my shoulder into the distance.

Gathering my courage, I turned around.

*Her eyes were a radiant and translucent blue.
They were filled with the kind of love I had
seen only in my soul. Beams of platinum light
shot from her outstretched hands and skipped
across the night. They illuminated the darkness
like exploding embers cast from an enormous
fire. She smiled at me, and her love was
delivered directly into my heart.*

♥

Sixty One

Only about three years old, a little girl stood in a swirling cloud of violet and silver light. Her face emerged and then disappeared in the magnificent light. Her blond hair and features were mine when I had been small. Her body was transparent, and in it I could see her heart turning rapidly like a waterwheel fed by a rushing stream. Glorious colors of gold, lilac, pink, and blue spun in her heart in a display of awesome beauty.

Her eyes were a radiant and translucent blue. They were filled with the kind of love I had seen only in my soul. Beams of platinum light shot from her outstretched hands and skipped across the night. They illuminated the darkness like exploding embers cast from an enormous fire. She smiled at me, and her love was delivered directly into my heart.

I heard a deep, rumbling that sounded like distant thunder. The stars in the sky directly above her began to move slowly toward one another like ancient friends.

Feeling both excited and terrified, I cried. "What's happening?" No one answered. The two girls who lived inside me seemed equally stricken with awe.

The magical three-year-old smiled up at the sky, and the stars coalesced into a bright silver oval almost as big as the moon. Then, the phenomenon slowly moved toward us. As it came closer, I could see slow whirls of sparkling rose and green moving inside it. Then, a soft voice began to sing a timeless melody of boundless love. The song wrapped around me, and I knew there was only one place I wanted to go.

The child sent out streams of light from her hands and created a glorious pathway of silver up into the sky. She turned toward me and smiled again. Then, she waved me forward. Mesmerized, I followed the magnificent three-year-old up the mysterious incandescent trail.

Sixty Two

S uddenly, a great light burst over the pathway. An immense wave of joy swept over us, and we were carried even higher into the sky. Now, the little girl gazed into the darkness above her, an ecstatic expression on her small face.

A glorious man slowly materialized out of the emptiness, and I could see that we were safely held within his cupped hands. His luminous smile revealed limitless devotion, and his sweet breath wafted over us like a breeze on a warm night. He whispered, "Oh, my dear ones, you are so loved." The child's heart immediately began to spin faster, and the energy around us became even more beautiful. She giggled with delight and skipped in circles. Incandescent splashes of energy went flying over my head.

Overwhelmed by an almost incomprehensible love, I whispered, "You're my soul." It wasn't a question; this resplendent being couldn't be anyone else.

"He's *our* soul," the child said reverently. She had stopped moving, and now looked up at him, her eyes filled with absolute love. Very gently, he lifted her up so that she could lean against his face. Clearly feeling totally safe, she nestled near his shimmering cheek.

A cascade of questions began to flood my mind. I decided to go with the most obvious one. "Who is she?"

"Your divine child," my soul answered.

"I don't understand."

"Every human being has within him or herself a divine child. It is the place where spirit first touches matter."

"I can see our soul all the time!" the child cried. She caressed the face of the one who had made us, and added, "I try to visit all the children who live inside you. I want to make sure they never forget about him."

In wonder, I said, "You can travel back and forth between our soul and the girls I just met?"

"If I watch carefully, sometimes I can find a way to get into your heart. Then, I can talk to the other kids."

I immediately knew what she meant. "But a lot of the time, my heart's too full of density. You can't get in because there's not enough room."

"You've got to be careful about that," she chastised gently. "When you don't talk to your little kids, and I can't talk to them, they get pretty sad and upset."

I thought a moment. "Why can't they see our soul like you can?"

"The divine child in each person is not encumbered by density," my soul replied. "Yours managed to grow to be three years old before density invaded your heart. After that, all the inner children were plagued with it."

"And that makes them too heavy to be able to see you?" I said, feeling terribly sad. After all, those children were so innocent. If anyone had a right to be in intimate contact with our soul, they did!

His answer wasn't comforting. "They are caught in density. Your divine child seeks to remind them of me, but it is up to you to free them so that they can be with me."

"And I free them by getting rid of the density." My statement came with a sense of resignation. No matter how I looked at it, clearing out my own density seemed to be the key to everything. My soul couldn't save me from my own choices. Nobody was going to rescue me. I had to do the work of releasing myself.

"Tell me some more about my divine child," I pleaded.

"Your life began when I sent my energy into your body," he answered. "In that moment, the divine child was born. She lives on Earth, but she can travel to be with me. That is how you were meant to live throughout your lifetime. Once density entered your heart, and the social mind developed, most of you have remained earthbound. Still, your divine child is free."

"Is everyone's divine child the same age as mine is?"

"No," he said sadly. "Most of them are much younger than three. It depends on how long it took for density to find its way into a person's heart. Some divine children are only infants."

"How can I make contact with her? How can anybody reach their own divine child?"

"Ah," my soul smiled. "That is the purpose of the tenth energy."

I grinned as a wonderful sense of hope surged in my heart. "You're talking about what we call Sagittarius, right?"

He nodded. "During this special time each year, we send the energy of the divine child over the Earth. You are reminded of the exuberance and joy that belong to this important aspect of yourself. You have a chance to tap into that invigorating sense that the world is clean and new, and you are, too. You can break free of all that holds you back. Embrace the world with supreme confidence—the kind that comes from the unsullied innocence of the young."

"It sounds like we have a chance to dump the past and start fresh!"

My soul smiled again. "The doorway to all the spiritual realms is in the present. By focusing your attention on the moment at hand, you have the chance to fuse together the energies of spirit with those on Earth. Then, you can live as you were meant to, with your feet on the ground, and your head in the heavens."

"I guess I don't have to ask what the symbol for the tenth energy is," I said happily. "It has to be a beautiful child."

"So it is," my soul replied. "Let go of everything that holds you down. Release your shame and guilt. Absolve yourself of your mistakes. Forgive and clean your heart continually. Allow the gift of love to enter your life. Those are the lessons of the divine child."

Something amazing galloped across my mind. "That's why Daniel first appeared to me as a little boy! A presence like him exists within each of us! We carry our own wonderful teachers deep inside our hearts."

My divine child giggled uproariously. "Oh Karen," she cried. "Sometimes, it takes you so long to figure things out!"

In that moment, I felt gloriously free and intensely alive. My heart could be infused with the effervescent joy of my divine child any time I allowed it to happen. I renewed my dedication to cleaning myself of density. Now I had an inspired reason to do it. There were innocent children inside of me. They deserved to be free. All the different parts of me had a right to look into the loving eyes of our soul.

Then I realized that the place I was standing was my own heart. That heart existed within the loving hands of my soul. Even if I never acknowledged it, even if I became so confused that I didn't believe in a soul, even if I filled my heart with density, still my soul loved me and supported my life.

The divine child leaped from her position near our soul's face and embraced me. Suddenly, I was surrounded with many beautiful children. Although they were different ages, each one looked like me. Their faces sent out rays of platinum light, and their bodies glowed from a source deep inside. Our soul poured his love down over us, and we were filled with his light. Ever so gently, he touched the heart within each child with a luminous fingertip, until we were all delirious with joy.

As though he heard the call of something undeniable, my soul suddenly became absolutely still. His radiance began to build, until it was no longer containable. Waves of ecstasy rolled past his boundaries and illuminated the space far beyond him. Then, with a burst of blinding white light, someone even greater than my soul arrived. Overwhelmed by the increasing energy, I fell into a state of indescribable bliss. Very near me, a voice whispered:

"Through the secret door within your heart, you have journeyed to my home. My beloved child, know that you are forever welcome. Rejoice, and enter now. Come, and be with me."

Sixty Three

"Here outside the cycles of time, and the containment of space, your heart has broken through the wall of illusion and now soars far beyond the sky. That heart was born in the realm of angels and has again arrived to be with them."

In an ecstatic daze, I heard the voice speak to me with indescribable love. White heat burned away my senses, yet my ability to perceive increased ten thousand fold. Ignited with a passionate energy of almost unbearable intensity, my being grew far faster than the speed of light, until it extended over the universe. The stars shimmered and spun in the vast spaces within me. My heart dwarfed the sun and burst with an urgent desire to reunite with something that was beyond form, beyond beauty, beyond imagination.

My bliss was bordering on ecstatic agony, yet energy continued to shoot through me. Now it began to increase in power and duration. It seemed I would surely be blown apart. Still, I went toward its source, certain I wanted nothing but to drown myself in that love.

"You can't have too deep of contact with me and still remain on the Earth. My light will dissolve your existence away before your time is through. Even in ecstasy you shall not see me, yet you can know me while in the arms of your soul."

"My love has created your heart, and in the end, you will return that heart to me. Set yourself ablaze and rejoice in the fire—burn everything away that is not of love. For only love can ever come home to me."

"Do not allow yourself to fall into senseless sleep but keep careful watch under both stars and sun. For my love travels within a million disguises, and out of the silence, my messages arrive unannounced."

"Become an empty container so that I may fill you with my light and remember that even one bright lantern can lead all people home. For one filled with love is enough to illuminate the darkness, as sure as the sun makes beautiful the stars and moon."

"Just as the drop of dew will eventually find its way to the sea, so you cannot help but return to me. Therefore, leave behind your fear, and ardently fall into your lover's bed. Unashamed, gaze into the eyes of your soul, and offer him everything. For when it is time, the Earth and sky will unite as one. And all souls whom I set in motion; I will call home."

"Now I return you to your form. Go upon the Earth and release my words. Watch them fly across all lands and then go heavenward and return to my heart again. All things flow in and out of me and so do not grieve. Send your heart across the land, the sea, the skies...and know always, you shall be forever and ever, deeply loved."

Sixty Four

Completely exhausted, I lay sobbing on warm sand. The gentle lapping of water reassured me that I was safe back on the Earth.

"Don't even start to think about it, Karen." I heard the familiar little voice off to my left.

"Daniel?" I croaked. "Do you have any idea where I've just been?"

"Sure," he said happily. I opened one eye and found him sitting beside me, a cheerful grin on his face. Clad in bright purple swimming trunks, his blond hair blew in the breeze. I decided to sit up and saw that we were on a very small island in the midst of an azure sea. A single palm tree struggled to offer a patch of shade.

Feeling like the proverbial ship-wrecked sailor, I asked, "Where are we?"

"On Earth," the little boy replied. "Want something to eat?" Before I could answer, he brought a picnic basket from behind his back. "Here," he said, as he extended a cold bottle of mineral water. "At least have something to drink."

"How do you do these things?" As soon as the question came out of my mouth, I withdrew it with a wave of my hand. After what I had just been through, apparently anything was possible. The universe was made of pure magic—there was no use in attempting to figure it out.

Looking far into the distance, I could see only more water. "Why are we on this little island, Daniel?"

"Just wanted to show you one more time," he said with a giggle.

"Show me what?"

He frowned a little with consternation. "You've got to try

harder, Karen! This tiny island is like where you usually place your consciousness. After you've explored your little space, you get depressed because there's nothing wonderful about it. You get frustrated and mad because you feel trapped. But look! You're always surrounded by something enormous and full of life. The ocean is like the field of energy that is your soul. Jump in! Don't wait for a boat to come and save you. Don't look to the outside for someone to come along and release you from your confinement. Learn how to swim! Learn how to plunge right into the beauty all around you."

"I have to ask," I said shakily. "Was that who I think it was?"

"Who?" he said innocently. He busied himself in the picnic basket and finally produced an enormous piece of watermelon. "Want some?"

I was terrified to voice what I was thinking. "Daniel, was that God?"

"You're thinking too much," he warned. "Once you get a label for what happened, then you're going to kill your experience. You'll get it all boxed up and figured out, and it'll be absolutely dead." He paused and took a big bite out of the watermelon. "That's the whole problem with religions. They try to talk about things that won't fit into words, or even your ability to reason. Pretty soon, people think that a symbolic reference to the divine is a literal truth. Once that happens, there's no room in the symbol for anything divine. It's just a dead reference to something that's alive, and beyond words."

I opened my mouth to beg him to answer my question, but he jumped in and continued to talk. "Remember, the brain limits your understanding of reality. The only way to perceive the divine is through your heart. Your mind will never bring you any closer to God."

"See, the laws of thinking determine what you can think. The important stuff's way bigger than your capacity to think. If you keep trying, pretty soon you'll have to get what you've seen into a tiny box that the laws of thinking can deal with. Then, you'll lose all the good parts."

I suddenly thought about a poem I had read a long time ago. William Blake wrote:

> *"He who binds to himself a joy*
> *Does the winged life destroy;*
> *But he who kisses the joy as it flies*
> *Lives in eternity's sunrise."*

Some things weren't meant to be nailed down, categorized, explained, or filed safely away. There are moments in life when all your beliefs tumble to the floor, and you're faced with choosing madness or transformation. I had to accept what I'd experienced and then allow myself to draw my strength from it. Life was never going to be the same. I could never go back to believing that anything was what it appeared to be. The truth seemed to be that all things had multiple layers of meaning, purpose, and origin. Before I met Daniel, I had traveled only across the outer levels of reality. Now, I had the capacity to dive deeper. I knew that there were countless dimensions to our existence. I could choose how, and where, I wanted to live.

I remembered a Buddhist teaching I had once come across. It said: "The highest stage of realization is the exhaustion of phenomenal reality." Now I realized what it meant. We had to keep shedding our understandings, until we had nothing left but a vision of unbroken love. Everything was made of love; any perception that deviated from that was only an illusion, meant to be cast aside. Doubt about the spiritual nature of things was only the social mind's desperate attempt to defend itself from reality. Doubt left us nothing to believe in, nothing to hope for, and nothing to live by.

"Yep," Daniel interrupted gleefully. "That's it! That's how the whole thing works. Just ignore the personality's alarms. They only go off when you're right on the edge of transformation."

I smiled at him and took his little hand in mine. Sticky with fruit juice, it was so innocent, yet so strong. "Can I just ask you one question?" I said softly.

"You want to know about what he meant when he said, 'the Earth and the sky will become as one,' huh?"

My voice came out in a whisper. "Does that refer to the end of the world, Daniel? There are a lot of people who are convinced that the millennium will bring a total destruction of the planet."

"Oh, human beings always get really worried at the thousand year marks!" he said, giggling. "There's no magic about a number. The fate of the Earth is up to all of you. There's no plan to rob you of your choice. You can destroy her and take away your wonderful opportunity to grow. Or you can clean away all of your density, and burst into freedom, just like the star of Bethlehem."

Suddenly, the child was surrounded by the luminous body of the adult Daniel. Light shot out from his eyes and hands, and his heart spun madly with beautiful energy. The little boy immediately entered that heart and splashed happily in the sparkling particles of rose and silver. The adult took my hands in his and said, "Remember, the second chance is just beginning. The walls between the dimensions are breaking down. Everywhere you look, there are healers, and spiritual helpers. The Earth is awash with the energy of love. Bathe yourselves in it; cherish the divine child who lives in your heart, and open that heart as wide as you can. Memories of your true nature will begin to come back to you, and a deep feeling of something homelike and uncannily familiar will awaken. Finally, gloriously, you will remember who you truly are and make your way home."

Tears rolled down my face, and I could think of only one thing to say. "Thank you, Daniel. Thank you so much for all you have given me."

"You're welcome," he said simply. Then he smiled broadly and added, "I have many things to tell you about when we meet again."

"There's more?" I said, feeling a rush of excitement. A favorite line from *Alice In Wonderland* poked up through my consciousness. "Daniel, things keep getting curiouser and curiouser!"

After looking at me for a long moment, he said very gently, "Oh, but we have just begun."

Thank You

I T TAKES TRUE COURAGE TO OPEN THE MIND and even more to cultivate peace in a world filled with uncertainty. As you reflect on what you've experienced, I invite you to take what resonates deeply with your heart—and let the rest fall away. This isn't about creating more dogma; it's about shedding light on a path that leads to healing, spiritual growth, and boundless curiosity.

If this book has touched you in any way, I would be so grateful if you would consider leaving a review. Your words can help spread the message, touching others who may be seeking the same peace and understanding.

Thank you, once again, for taking this journey with me.

About the Author

WHEN I WAS SIX, FATE TAPPED ME ON THE SHOULDER. My awareness became global. I was able to see things and know things which were inexplicable. I spent my childhood and teen years mostly alone. There was so much available to me I didn't have time for regular things.

When I was 27, I began to hear someone called Daniel. I am the last person to believe in spiritual guides or channeled teaching. I could not deny Daniel. He asked for nothing. He made himself available to anyone who wanted to listen and the interest grew.

My friend and I began to record his teachings and made the content available to others. I began writing books. Then Andi Saucerman arrived, another being created with the purpose of helping me get Daniel's message out into the world, and we took off. Life diverted us for a while. We each had a child. Andi began teaching for an organization dedicated to transformative adult education and spiritual growth.

Now we are back and ready to serve you.

Andi has formed Universoul Foundations as a vehicle to provide Daniel's teachings in books, online courses, webinars, in-person retreats and more for those who are ready to take the most exciting journey of all—the one straight into the heart of the soul.

About Universoul Foundations

A t Universoul Foundations, we are dedicated to helping you reunite—not just conceptually, but literally—with your own Soul. Through transformative books and courses, we guide you on a journey to rediscover your true self, reconnect with your higher purpose, and align with the abundant energy of love, creativity, and joy.

Our mission is simple: to serve humanity by sharing spiritual teachings that reunite you with your Soul, nurture inner peace, and empower you to live a life filled with purpose and abundance.

Through our offerings, you will come to understand your true essence. In doing so, you'll remember:

- Your divine, triune nature
- Your higher purpose on Earth
- The unconditional love of your Highest Self and Soul
- That we are all interconnected, united by love and light
- That God and humanity are one

To learn more please contact us at:

- *Email:* hello@universoulfoundations.com
- *Website: universoulfoundations.com*

Who is Daniel?

WHEN ASKED WHO HE IS, DANIEL TYPICALLY RESPONDS that he (or 'we' as he often uses during some teachings) is 'of spirit from beyond the beyond.' And although the name Daniel denotes male energy, Daniel is of both feminine and masculine energy—as we all are. In fact, Daniel's usual response to questions about who he is, is that it is much more important for us to understand who we are.

> *"Daniel is a mirror, with a voice,*
> *to remind you who you are.*
> *A messenger from the fabric of the infinite,*
> *a reflector of God."*

Those who have experienced Daniel speak of him as a gentle, loving spirit, with great compassion, seemingly limitless wisdom, and a wonderful sense of humor. Daniel has stated his purpose is to help each of us to reconnect with our own Soul. His mission is to infuse, imbibe, to bring back to our awareness who we are. By doing so, we can experience great joy and align ourselves again with our purpose for being on Earth.

Topics that Daniel discusses include both physical and spiritual issues, such as life beyond death, spiritual growth, the power of love, healthy living, understanding relationships, Soul contracts, the spiritual structure of physical existence, knowing God/Goddess/All That Is, extraterrestrials and UFO's, humanity's influences on Gaia, and much, much more.

Reconnect to the Truth of Who You Are

FREE PDF DOWNLOAD

Are you ready to learn more from Daniel? These free offerings will guide you to a deeper understanding of who you truly are and why you are here.

- **Beloved:** Open your heart to the infinite love and patience that your soul has always held for you.

- **Follow Your Own Soul:** Learn the power of what happens if you create a tiny opening for spirit to flow through you.

By signing up for these free teachings, you'll also receive our exclusive weekly newsletter—packed with spiritual insights, practical wisdom, and powerful offerings designed to help you tap into the boundless love and energy of your soul. You can unsubscribe at any time.

Download your free PDFs now at:
https://www.universoulfoundations.com/free-offerings